ORANGE BLOSSOM SPECIAL

SALLY KILPATRICK

NYLA Publishing

121 W 27th St., Suite 1201, New York, NY 10001

http://www.nyliterary.com

"Kilpatrick gives us a deep, fully realized and believable romance."
--Nashville Bookworm on *Bittersweet Creek*

For Peter
Thanks for taking a chance on me
Oh, and sorry I included the hearse again

ACKNOWLEDGMENTS

Thanks to my husband, Ryan, for his continued support even when I insist on writing about hearses and saying things like "it's like *Thelma & Louise* meets *As I Lay Dying*." Thanks to my kids, even if they like to "explore" the attic or play video games while I'm trying to write. Much gratitude to Tanya, Mom, Laura, Jenni, and anyone else who put eyeballs on my little novella. Special thanks to author and historian Jack Neely who confirmed many facts about Knoxville for me—if you haven't tried his books, you should. Finally, thanks to Zachary from Hearseclub who identified the make and model of the Orange Blossom Special and told me not only how to break her down but also how to build her back up. Finally, thanks to my agent Sarah Younger for everything, but especially helping me get this novella back on the road.

As everyone had long feared, it was Tennessee football that finally killed Jerome Malcolm. Sure, the death certificate said *"cardiac arrest,"* but an anemic Tennessee offense and the wily Steve Spurrier were truly to blame. Edie, his wife, consoled herself with the fact that her husband had gone peacefully in his sleep—even if it was after two hours of ranting and raving about the inadequacies of the Tennessee offense—and that he hadn't suffered from dementia, a broken hip, or the indignities of the nursing home.

She and Jerome celebrated their sixtieth wedding anniversary the month before, and she'd officially forgotten what life was like before Jerome came stomping in with his huge feet, infectious laugh, and propensity for waltzing with her in the kitchen when no one else was looking. As husbands went, he really only had two faults: his addiction to Tennessee football and a tendency to do household chores for his sister before his wife.

"Oh, Edie. You handle a hammer better than I do," he would say.

And this was true, but not the point, so she would reply,

"Yes, but I also handle the washer, dryer, dishwasher, and vacuum better than you do."

Edie looked around her kitchen and wiped away a tear at the thought that there would be no more impromptu waltzes for her. Probably best, since she had no intention of breaking a hip and ending up in a nursing home—not if she could help it. No, she had a bottle of pills with her name on it. She'd get out of this world while the getting was good, just as soon as she took care of Jerome.

She paused and misted up because, if she pretended hard enough, she could almost imagine Jerome barreling through that swinging door and taking her into his arms as he began to hum "The Blue Danube." The kitchen certainly looked almost the same as when they'd moved into the cozy brick ranch back in the fifties: oak cabinets, now faded laminate countertops, and dingy tile with a sunny disposition. Like Edie, the kitchen was worn but well-maintained.

She cut off two more hunks of the pineapple cake and told herself to quit stalling. The lawyer was there to read the will, and she wanted the whole thing over with so she could mourn in peace. She didn't care one whit about Jerome's earthly possessions.

Balancing a dessert plate in each hand, she hobbled her way through the swinging door and into the dour dining room that Jerome had always hated. *"Fussy and stiff,"* he'd called it. Well, Edie still liked the old Duncan Phyfe dinette set she'd argued for when they first married. When she pointed out that she easily earned half of all the money they made, Jerome had good-naturedly thrown his hands in the air and told her to go for it. He'd been different from her friends' husbands like that.

She set the larger slice of cake in front of Peyton and carried her own to the seat at the end of the table. The *clink* of forks on plates and cups on saucers were the only sounds for a few minutes before Walter, her teenage grandnephew, finally spoke. "This cake is really good, Aunt Edie. Thank you."

Edie couldn't help but notice that her sister-in-law, Janice, glared at her grandson as if he were a traitor. Edie smiled. "Thank you, Walter. I'm glad you're enjoying it."

"It is quite good. I don't often get such a treat when I read a will," said Ben Little, the lawyer at the other end of the table.

"Well, I'm happy to oblige, Mr. Little."

"Now, now, Miss Edie. I thought we'd discussed how you can call me Ben."

"If that's the case, then you'll have to drop the 'miss.'"

"Touché."

Edie liked Ben Little and was so glad she'd sent Jerome to his practice when he started clamoring about making a will. She'd taught high school with Ben's grandmother back when they finally integrated the schools. The two women had become fast friends, both outcasts in their own ways. Edie was a Yankee and persona non grata at the faculty lunch table for being an outsider with blunt ways. Elvira Little had skin a shade darker than bronze and hailed from the "other" school, one that many of the teachers saw as separate but most certainly not equal.

By the time Ben had graduated from law school, race relations around town had improved considerably, but it still took him a while to build a clientele. Jerome was one of his first customers, and from there Ben had built his practice one happy client at a time. He'd never needed Edie's help, but he always seemed to appreciate it nonetheless, and she appreciated his attention to detail and how kind he'd been since Jerome's passing.

As the odd group ate their cake and sipped on either coffee or milk, Edie studied those who had been named in Jerome's will. Peyton, a skinny redheaded teenager, lived next door, but she spent a lot of time with Edie and Jerome. Edie had the idea that life wasn't too great in the trailer next door. She never turned the girl away, and she always made sure to feed her.

Next to Peyton sat Janice. She and Jerome had been particularly close as brother and sister, so close that Edie had lost the argument when she'd suggested that maybe it wouldn't be a good idea to have Janice living next door. Nope. Instead she'd endured almost daily the subtle insinuation that she'd only married Jerome for his money.

The fourth beneficiary of the will was one of Janice's grand-children, Walter. He was the youngest of her grandchildren, the son of one of the daughters she'd adopted from Africa. Walter spent a lot of time with Janice, doing the things her husband, Harvey, could no longer do, like mow the lawn. He always mowed Edie's lawn, too, without being asked. All he ever wanted in return was something from her pie safe and to be able to watch football on the big screen with Jerome.

Maybe she should give that television to Walter.

But then the kids wouldn't come over anymore.

Edie, you're not going to be here for the kids to come over.

Edie pushed away the cake she no longer had any taste for, her stomach somewhere near her toes.

"Everyone ready?"

"Please proceed, Mr. Little."

"Let me summarize what I read," Ben was saying. "The house, the property over in Cleburne County, and almost all of Mr. Malcolm's investments go to his wife, but—"

"Of course they do," Janice said bitterly. "She's been waiting for them."

"Janice, I think sixty years of marriage means I'm officially not a gold digger, and the next time you imply it, I'm going to throw wild onions in your yard. And pick my dandelions and blow all of their little seeds in your general direction."

Janice gasped. Her lawn was a perfectly maintained carpet of zoysia, and she babied it and all of her landscaping as if her life depended on it.

"Aw, Aunt Edie, please don't do that," Walter said.

Edie sighed. She couldn't do that to Walter, since he did all of the mowing and worked as his grandmother's assistant, helping her prune the crepe myrtles and such. "For you, Walter, I won't." She turned to Janice. "But I don't want to hear that word ever again or I'll park the Orange Blossom Special in *your* driveway."

Janice narrowed her eyes at Edie. The one thing both Edie and Janice could agree on was that they both hated the old hearse that had been painted in an orange-and-white checkerboard to be Jerome's "ultimate tailgating machine." Edie would get a kick out of parking the hearse over at Janice's and letting it leak oil all over her pristine driveway.

"Speaking of the, ah, Orange Blossom Special," Ben said, "it's going to be important in just a few minutes."

That got everyone's attention so he could carry on. "Mr. Malcolm redesignated some funds a few years before. He put aside a little travel fund for both of you, Miss Janice and Miss Edie. He said he hoped the two of you would go to Hawaii together, since you both said you wanted to go, and he wasn't about to get on a plane himself."

When hell freezes over, Edie thought. Janice's face contorted into a similar expression. But that was Jerome, always saying things like, "I swear the two of you would actually get along pretty well if you'd cut out the petty nonsense."

"He also set aside a couple of college funds, for Peyton and Walter, at a hundred thousand each."

"Oh," Edie said. She and Jerome had had separate checking and savings accounts since the eighties, and she had no idea he'd had that kind of money. Of course, they'd always saved a heckuva lot more than they'd spent and she knew he liked to play with his stocks. He'd seemed pretty happy about that Home

Depot stock he'd bought so long ago. Maybe she should've paid more mind.

Edie felt Janice's glare and knew that it was killing the woman not to lob her favorite insult, but she loved her newly pressure-washed driveway too much to risk it. Edie had never wanted Jerome's money, but if she had a dollar for every time Janice had called her a gold digger? Well, she'd be rich enough not to ever need it.

Ben turned to the younger people. "Peyton, Walter, you may have these funds to go to the college of your choice—although Mr. Malcolm may have mentioned a partiality for the University of Tennessee—as long as you comply with his wishes for disposing of his remains in the specific way he has requested."

Peyton's already pale face grew even whiter. "I don't like dead people, Mr. Little."

"Don't worry, he's been cremated and his ashes are in that, um, cookie jar over there, dear," Janice said, pointing to the sideboard, where a ceramic likeness of Carmen Miranda sat.

Peyton shivered in revulsion despite Carmen's smile and cheerful fruit hat.

Edie rolled her eyes. The Carmen Miranda cookie jar had been another of Jerome's requests. He loved to talk about the time he'd seen Carmen Miranda at some USO event. He loved even more to tease Edie about it because he knew she got jealous that she wasn't as curvy. Just when she'd thought he'd forgotten all about the Brazilian bombshell, he'd come in with that ridiculous cookie jar.

"And what do you expect me to do with that?" she'd asked.

"Put my ashes in it so I can finally commune with Carmen," he'd said.

That had been four or five years ago, and she could thank Target for making the cookie jar and bringing up the lady with the fruit hat once more. She'd thought her husband was kidding about the cookie jar, but he'd apparently made arrangements with Ben, so there he sat, communing with his precious Carmen at long last.

"Miss Edie?" Ben asked. "May we continue?"

"Of course."

"The four of you are to travel together in the Orange Blossom Special and to spread Mr. Malcolm's ashes evenly in three different places: the Ryman Auditorium, General Neyland's grave, and the checkerboard end zone at Neyland Stadium."

"Is that all?" Edie rolled her eyes. Her husband was a nut. Well, he had been a nut.

"You know I don't think you even miss him," Janice said, her voice hitching. "The way you're acting proves my point that you never really loved Jerome. Otherwise you would be willing to do whatever he asked you to do."

Too far, Janice.

"I loved Jerome Malcolm more than you will ever comprehend," she said, thinking of the bottle of pills that would allow her to join him as soon as she finished this wild-goose chase. Once she found her words, she continued in a voice dangerously low and cultivated from over thirty years of teaching high school math. "I am happy that he went the way he wanted to go, but in a few days, you'll all be gone and I'll be left alone with nothing but his memory. Don't presume to tell me how much I did or did not love my husband."

The women glared at each other in silence.

Peyton was the first to speak, as she started to pull away from the table. "This is all real nice of Mr. Malcolm, but I can't do it."

"Don't be silly." Walter put a hand on Peyton's arm to encourage her to sit back down. "It's enough money to get a college education. Can't you take a little car trip for that?"

She sat back down but still looked as though she might toss her cookies at any moment, and Edie's anger dissipated as she wondered what possibly could have spooked the girl so badly. Peyton's hands shook, but she took them from the top of the table and put them in her lap when she noticed Edie staring.

"Know what? You have a funny way of showing how much you supposedly loved my brother," Janice said again. She was sniffling now, and she reached into her pocketbook for a crumpled tissue to dab at her tears. Then she blew her nose with that distinctive honking sound that all the Malcolms seemed to make.

"We all mourn in our own ways," Edie said. "I'm not sure I've even begun to grieve yet."

The oppressive *tick*ing of the clock might as well have been a bass drum for how well it punctuated the sudden silence. Edie would have to remember to start winding it. That had been Jerome's job.

Ben cleared his throat to regain their attention. "Mr. Malcolm's will also stipulated that, for this trip, Peyton and Walter are to take turns driving—"

"That's preposterous!" Janice and Edie said in unison.

"Awesome!" Walter held out a hand for Peyton to slap, but she wasn't as enthusiastic. She still looked a little green, to tell the truth.

"He, uh, didn't think either of you should be driving," Ben said apologetically to Edie and Janice. "Especially not the older car. He might have mentioned how you'd never make it to Knoxville if someone wasn't doing the speed limit."

"Well, I never," Edie said softly. Jerome had always been the one with the lead foot.

Ben shrugged. "He said, and I quote, 'The old girl needs to be aired out at least one more time.'"

Edie couldn't help but chuckle. *She* was an old girl who was about to be aired out one last time.

"I'm not riding in that hearse." Janice sat back and crossed her arms.

Edie wanted to caution her against wrinkling her linen suit, but instead she said, "Now look who doesn't love Jerome enough to follow his dying wish."

"Fine." Janice ground the word out between her teeth. "I will ride across the state in his ridiculous hearse that's been painted orange and white. There's nothing I would like more."

Ben tugged at his collar. "Upon the successful completion of this task, Peyton and Walter will each receive access to an account that has been specifically designated for their college education. Miss Edie and Miss Janice, you will, of course, receive access to your travel fund, and Miss Janice will also receive the family Bible."

Janice sucked in a breath.

Edie couldn't help but think, *So that's where it went.* Janice had been harping about that Bible for the past twenty years or better, carrying on about how it should've been passed on to her instead of to Jerome. Meanwhile, that sneaky man had hidden it somewhere to cash in for a favor later. Oh, her husband could be manipulative if he wanted to be.

"What's my incentive for going along with this harebrained scheme?" Edie asked. She wouldn't mind traveling with Walter and Peyton. Janice, however? She didn't want to spend fifteen minutes in a car with Janice, much less take a trip across the state with her.

Ben grinned. "He said you'd ask that question. He also said you'd go along with it out of the goodness of your heart."

Edie stabbed her pineapple cake and crammed a huge bite into her mouth. She wasn't feeling much "goodness in her heart" at the moment. Eating cake was better than giving in to the urge to stab something else, though. Or *someone*.

"He might've mentioned something about how you'd be able to take that trip to Paris."

Edie's fork hit her plate, and she tried hard to swallow over the lump in her throat. She'd given Jerome such grief over his unwillingness to fly. Now he was telling her to go on without him.

She thought of her bottle of pills. They'd still be there after a trip to Paris.

"He suggested you might want to sell the Orange Blossom Special to help pay for the trip," Ben added.

Damn straight, I'm going to sell that hunk of junk.

"Is the—Orange Blossom Special—a stick shift? I can't drive a stick shift," Peyton blurted.

Bless her heart. She was trying so hard to get out of this. If her parents caught wind of it, they'd make her go and then try to take the money for themselves. Edie hoped Jerome had written stipulations for that scholarship in such a way that they couldn't.

"I can teach you how," Walter said. "It's not that hard."

"Thanks," she said, but she still looked too green around the edges to exude any real gratitude.

Edie set her fork down on her plate. "Well, that seems to be all settled, then. Thank you, Mr. Little."

"Miss Edie," he said as he gathered up his belongings.

"When are we supposed to make this trip?" Janice said, her lips pursed as though she'd just eaten a lemon. She hadn't touched her piece of pineapple cake, either. It shouldn't have bothered Edie so much, but it did. Oh, it rankled. Never once had Janice tasted one of Edie's desserts.

"I'd recommend the Vanderbilt game," Ben said. "I didn't want to mention it yet, because I don't know for sure, but I have a friend who could possibly get you some tickets. It'd be in the Vanderbilt section, but they would be good seats. Oh, and I do have to warn you that scattering those ashes could be considered trespassing."

"Will you come bail us out, since it's for a noble cause?" Edie asked, only half-kidding.

Ben shifted his briefcase from one hand to the other. "I'm

afraid this is rather like *Mission: Impossible,* and I will have to disavow any knowledge of your actions other than to say that I read the will."

Edie sighed. It was just like Jerome to send them all on an impossible mission. She could almost hear him humming the theme song.

2

By the Thursday before the Tennessee–Vanderbilt game, Janice had reconciled herself to the fact that she was about to drive across the state with her brother's dead ashes in an ancient hearse painted orange and white. She wasn't excited about sharing the backseat with Edie, however.

Money-grubbing heifer.

Okay, so Edie wasn't after Jerome's money. Janice knew better, but it had become a habit over the years.

For the life of her, she'd never been able to see what her brother had seen in that stick-figured, knock-kneed, sharp-tongued woman who obviously didn't want children. He'd met her at the University of Tennessee and then dragged her all the way across the state to torment them all.

He should've sent her back up North where she belonged.

Now, Janice. Obviously there was something he liked about her.

One day, a couple of years after he and Edie had married, Jerome had been over to fix her air conditioner. He took a long swig of tea and looked her dead in the eye. "I don't know why you have to give Edie such a hard time. You'd like her if you ever got to know her."

She snorted. All these years later, and she still didn't know how to get to know her sister-in-law. She was a Yankee, for starters. Claimed she came from Pennsylvania, but she'd never once talked about who her mama and daddy were. Then there was the fact that Edie had actually traveled. Janice had never been any farther than Memphis. They couldn't talk children because Edie thought she was too good to have any, all self-righteous women's libber. Heck, if they were to ever argue about it, Janice would've become tongue-tied because she never went to college and didn't have any of Edie's fancy words. Best she could tell, she'd never needed them, either.

"Sissy," Jerome had said, using his old pet name. "Can't you try to be a little nicer?"

So she'd tried at the very next holiday, which happened to be a family picnic for Labor Day. Janice had volunteered to make the potato salad, and Edie took the bowl from her saying, "Oh!"

"Oh, what?' Janice said suspiciously.

"I'm used to potato salad being warm," Edie said.

Well, here in the South, it's cold," she'd snapped.

In retrospect, she probably shouldn't have snapped at Edie. She'd since learned that there was a German potato salad that was served warm, but at the time it had felt as though Edie was looking for one more thing to criticize. At the beginning, she'd clipped her words really closely, too, but Janice had to admit that Edie's accent was softer and slower, rounder.

Janice studied herself in the bathroom mirror. Softer, slower, and rounder. She could be talking about herself. She turned sideways and tried to suck in her gut, but the control-top panty hose was doing all it could do. For heaven's sake, she didn't know what to wear to all of these places they were going. She would've asked Harvey, but he didn't know any better than she did.

She patted the bleach-blond locks she'd shellacked into

place. All she needed to do now was touch up her lipstick, and she'd be as ready for this trip as she could be.

"Are you almost done in there?" Edie asked from the other side of the door. "I'd like to get started before sundown, and we all need to pee before we start on this crazy trip."

So rude.

So crude.

Janice blotted her lipstick and waited a few seconds more, just to irritate her sister-in-law.

"About time," Edie grumbled as she brushed past Janice wearing elastic-waistband slacks and a plain shirt. Janice felt a twinge of guilt when she noticed both Peyton and Walter were waiting in the hall, as well. Nah. They could take it. They had those young bladders.

Ten minutes later, they all stood in the driveway looking at the infamous Orange Blossom Special. The heavy, old-fashioned hearse was a late-fifties model Cadillac, complete with fins. Jerome had bought it from Dec Anderson a few months before and then had it painted in an orange-and-white-checkerboard pattern.

"Look at this," he'd said excitedly when he got it back from the detailers, "You have plenty of room for your grill, your cooler, and your luggage—*and* you can still fit five people in the two front seats. It's a genius idea for tailgating."

Edie and Janice had been listening to this speech together, and Edie had mumbled something about how it was his money if he wanted to spend it that way.

"Heck, I think you could get all that in there and still have room to take a nap!"

Janice shuddered at the memory of his saying that. Didn't he realize that most passengers of the old vehicle had been on their way to a dirt nap? Her brother had always been turned a little different.

"Well, the day's not getting any longer," Edie said, as she made for the driver's seat. "Let's get started."

"Oh no," Janice heard herself say. "If we're going to do this, we're going to do it right. Hand those keys over to one of the kids."

"Fine. Shotgun."

"Miss Edie, ma'am? I sometimes get carsick in the backseat," Peyton said.

"Okay, then. Kiddies up front. Biddies in the back."

Janice started to object to being called a biddie, but Edie had already slid into her seat behind the driver.

"Pitch me the keys," Walter said.

"Why?" Peyton held the keys to her chest.

"I'm driving."

"Why do you get to drive first?" Peyton asked. "It's because you're the one with the penis, isn't it?"

"No, I thought I was being *nice* and *chivalrous*," Walter said, "but if you want to drive this old boat so badly, then you go to it."

"Fine."

"Fine."

"Both of you get your cute little butts into the hearse and get this trip started," Edie said. "The sooner we get started, the sooner we'll get done."

Janice huffed, but she slid behind Walter, and Peyton rounded the car to take the wheel. She laid her arm on the armrest with a sigh, only to realize it wasn't the armrest. No, Edie had belted the Carmen Miranda cookie jar into the middle seat. Fitting, since Jerome was now back in the same spot as he was when he was alive: centered between the two of them.

3

*P*eyton's first thought was, *OMG, I'm driving a hearse.*

Her heart pounded against her rib cage, and she wondered if she could ever tell the other folks in the car why she'd wanted to drive. She felt really bad about being mean to Walter. He'd blushed when she said it was because he was the one with the penis, and she could kick herself because she liked him. Maybe, she even *liked* him, liked him. She didn't know why she'd said it, other than the panic she'd felt at having to sit in the car. She'd thought that maybe, just maybe, driving would distract her enough to keep her from freaking out.

When she was little bitty, her grandma had passed away after falling asleep in her recliner while watching *Wheel of Fortune,* and Peyton had been too young to know how to call her parents. She had, however, known to call 911. The police officers and firemen had all been so nice to her and complimented her on being so smart as to call them, but then there was a fire two blocks over and a bad wreck on the highway. They left her in the care of Hollis Anderson because no one could find her parents and her grandma hadn't needed the ambulance—that much was clear.

She remembered sitting in the middle seat of the hearse, snatching glances over her shoulder at the white-shrouded stretcher where her grandma lay under the sheet. Every now and again, the stretcher would lurch, making creaking and clicking noises that made her jump. She was too young to sit in the front seat with Mr. Anderson, who seemed to be carrying on a conversation with someone she couldn't see, and she really hated sitting in the middle by herself.

When they got to the funeral home, Mr. Anderson took her by the hand and led her to the kitchen, where Miss Caroline had found some cookies and a Sprite for her. At first, she'd thought she wouldn't be able to swallow, but they tasted very good, and it gave her something to do other than think about how her grandma was gone.

Then Mr. Anderson had come back and told her that her grandma had said to tell her that she was a very good girl and that she was sorry to have left her. Then he'd told her that Grandma had said, "Peyton May, I want you to make something of yourself. Don't fritter away your life the way your mother has."

Peyton had always wondered how Mr. Anderson could've possibly known that her grandma called her Peyton May. It had been their little secret, and her grandma was the only person she allowed to use her middle name. Any time her mother tried to, Peyton would wait until the woman was high and then steal money from the cigar box in the closet or cut up the curtains.

She was too old to cut up curtains now. That was for sure.

Peyton's eyes darted to the rearview mirror, and to the cookie jar where Mr. Jerome's ashes sat. She missed Mr. Jerome. He'd been so funny and so smart about football. Him and Miss Edie had a house that actually smelled nice, and they always had plenty of food. She didn't want to think about how Mr. Jerome was gone and Miss Edie was already older than her grandma had been. Peyton tried to swallow the lump in her throat. What was she supposed to do when the inevitable happened to Miss Edie?

"Peyton, dear. I could really use a break to, ah, powder my nose," Miss Janice said.

"You didn't go back at the house, did you?" Miss Edie asked. "You spent all your time in there primping, and I don't remember hearing a flush."

Miss Janice sighed. "Fine. I forgot. What about that Cracker Barrel over there? The one in Jefferson has nice restrooms, and maybe this one will, too."

Peyton guided the hearse down the exit. They'd barely been on the road for an hour.

"All right, this time everyone pees," Miss Edie said in her schoolteacher voice. "Young bladder, old bladder, I don't care. 'Pee while you can' will be our mantra for this trip. Got it?"

Miss Janice wrinkled her nose, but everyone left the car and did what Miss Edie said. Afterward, Peyton considered buying a Coke in a glass bottle, but she was afraid to have to pee before anyone else, so she went out on the porch instead. Walter joined her.

"I'm sorry for how I acted earlier," she said. "Hearses make me nervous."

Why had she said that?

"Why do hearses make you nervous?" Walter asked.

She shrugged, not ready to tell her story. "You can drive if you want to."

His head cocked to one side, he studied her as if seeing her for the first time. He'd generally ignored her when they watched football together with Mr. Jerome. He opened his mouth as though about to press her, but Miss Edie and Miss Janice emerged.

"Let's go, kids! Time is money," Miss Eddie said.

Peyton offered the keys to Walter, but he shook his head.

About an hour later, she would wish she'd insisted that he drive.

***

"Peyton, darling. I really need to get something to drink. I'm parched," Miss Janice said.

"Or you have to pee again," Miss Edie said under her breath.

"Do you have to be so crude?"

"That's not crude. I could show you crude."

"Look, if you'd brought three children into this world, you'd be having trouble with your bladder, too."

"Oh fine. Use that as an excuse again, why don't you?"

"Stop it!" Peyton jerked the car off the interstate—and something popped? Cracked? She wasn't sure what was happening. She applied the brakes and the old boat slowed down, but panic set in as she realized that turning the steering wheel did nothing. She yanked to the left and then to the right. Then she let the steering wheel go all the way around. She barely stopped at the end of the ramp to let a pickup pass, then let the Caddy float at an odd angle into the parking lot of a sketchy-looking gas station.

"What the heck was that?" Miss Edie asked.

Peyton couldn't stop the tears from rolling down her cheeks. "I think I broke it."

"Broke it?"

"I think I broke the steering wheel, but I didn't mean to!" Peyton said with a hiccup. She wasn't going to cry. Nope. She was going to get out of this car and find a place to sit until she could get herself together.

Before she could run away, though, Miss Janice grabbed her arm. "I'm sure it wasn't on purpose. This is an old car. If you'll tell us what's wrong, we can fix it."

Her shoulders shook, and she couldn't make the words come out.

"It's okay." Walter pried the keys from her hand. She didn't realize they'd been cutting into her hand until he took them away from her.

Miss Janice led her away from the car to lean against the dingy wall by a rusted ice machine. She patted Peyton's shoulder like her grandmother used to do when she was little. "It's okay. I'm sure Edie would tell you to dry those tears, but sometimes you have to let them out. It's okay. It's not your fault."

"I—I—don't like hearses," Peyton said.

"Your grandmother," Miss Janice said softly. "I had forgotten all about that."

"You knew?"

"Oh honey. Everyone *knew*. Your mama was so strung out that no one could find you, and some folks were talking about getting Child Protective Services to take you away from her, because it had to have been so awful to have to ride to a strange place with a strange person with you being such a little thing. How old were you? Three?"

"I was four," Peyton said. It was easier to breathe. Her secret wasn't such a secret, and that was more of a relief than she would've imagined.

"You're a very brave girl for going along with this. It's a lot of money that I know you can use, but you're very brave."

Peyton's chest puffed out. She couldn't remember any time in her life when someone had called her brave.

"Now, I really do need to use the facilities. Do you think you'll be okay?"

Peyton swiped at the last of her tears and nodded. She could do this. She could finish this trip and maybe not waste her life. She'd forgotten about Mr. Anderson's words to her, words that she was supposed to believe had come from her grandmother.

She'd messed up a lot in school, but she could still do this. She could get back into that hearse and finish this trip so she could get out of Ellery and go to school and make something of herself.

Maybe.

$\mathcal{W}$alter couldn't tell for the life of him what was wrong with the car, but he did feel nervous being alone with Aunt Edie. She always seemed so . . . severe. Kinda like Professor McGonagall in those Harry Potter movies.

"I said, what do you think is wrong with the old girl?"

"Um, I don't know, Aunt Edie."

"Jerome would've known," she muttered.

"Peyton said something about the steering. How about I start the car and try to turn the wheel? You can tell me if the tires turn."

Edie nodded, and Walter started the car, pretending he knew what he was doing. His mom only let him drive the Prius, and starting the Cadillac was like going from a Shetland pony to a Clydesdale. Sure enough, the wheel turned freely. He didn't need Aunt Edie to tell him the wheels weren't turning.

He cut the engine and got out. "I think we're going to need a mechanic."

"Have it all figured out?" Grandma Janice asked as she came around the corner with a downcast Peyton behind her.

"Afraid not," Aunt Edie said.

"Oh. Well." Grandma Janice's brow was furrowed. "We need to figure it out, because I'm going to need to stop at the next gas station."

"What?"

Grandma Janice's voice lowered to a whisper. "I couldn't possibly use the restroom in there."

Aunt Edie stared at her sister-in-law, slack-jawed. "Are you kidding me?"

"I don't think it's been cleaned since the Nixon administration."

"Then you hover!" Aunt Edie's voice echoed off the gas station walls, and Peyton looked to Walter with wide eyes. He shrugged.

"Maybe I don't hover as well as I used to," Grandma Janice said, her hands on her hips. Of the four of them, she looked as though she were headed to a business meeting in her suit, hose, and high heels.

"Janice, this is absolutely ridiculous," Edie said. "Jerome told me stories about how the two of you didn't even have indoor plumbing until the late fifties. Surely a woman who grew up with an outhouse can handle a gas station bathroom."

"I said I will hold it."

The older ladies squared off.

"Well, you're the one always talking about how having babies means you can't hold things like you used to. Just so you know, this car isn't going anywhere until a mechanic examines it and probably not until he drags it off to fix it. Hell, we could be stuck here in"—she twirled around, looking for some indication of where they were—"Bucksnort. Yes, we could be stuck in Bucksnort, which appears to be a reasonable facsimile of hell."

"Fine," Grandma Janice turned on her heel and huffed back into the gas station.

Aunt Edie sagged against the car. "Walter, could you be a

dear and go ask whoever's working in the gas station to see if he knows where we could find a good mechanic?"

"Yes, ma'am," he said, glad to leave the old lady drama behind.

The bell above the door tinkled in welcome, but the man behind the cash register eyed him warily. Walter was as respectful as he could be, but he made a note to send Peyton on any such errands in the future.

With a few more "yessirs" than the guy deserved, he managed to talk the cashier into calling the nearest mechanic and went back outside to see what his companions were doing.

At first, he'd thought this trip was the golden ticket he'd been seeking. He had a small scholarship to play football at one of the local colleges, but he'd always wanted to play for Tennessee. If he could finish this crazy trip, then he still had time to apply to Tennessee and try out as a walk-on. Based on their kicking this season, he figured they could use him.

Maybe I could even try out for wide receiver.

The thought lingered in the back of his mind like the devil on his shoulder. His mother had told him he could play football, but he could only be a kicker because she was afraid he might get hurt. He'd had to argue long and hard to get that far, and he neglected to tell his mother that kickers sometimes got tackled, too. Sometimes they even tackled others, and he was known for not letting people get past him. In his four years on the high school team, no one had ever returned a kick for a touchdown from one of his kicks.

What would happen if they didn't finish this trip because the car broke down? Would he have to forfeit the money? End up going to Jefferson State? Man, he had to get away from his mother. She was suffocating him, and he didn't even know how to tell her that he was a good teenager. He didn't drink. He didn't do drugs. He kept his grades up—and he didn't cheat.

She'd texted to check up on him three times since they'd left that morning.

He needed that woman to lighten up!

He needed all of these women to lighten up! First, Grandma Janice having to pee every five seconds. Then Aunt Edie yelling at people and Peyton losing her mess over the car.

Sweet Jesus, was that another woman?

Sure enough, one of the two people who'd emerged from the tow truck was a woman.

She whistled. "That's a pretty Caddy. Guy here at the gas station mentioned you've got a problem with it?"

"Pitman arm," said the man beside her, a tall man with a gray beard.

"Daddy, can you let the folks talk?" she asked.

Walter couldn't figure out how old she was or what she was all about. Bronze skin, not-quite-Southern accent except for the "daddy." He had to admit she was very pretty, her dark hair slicked back into a glossy ponytail.

Peyton told them in a halting voice about what had happened when she'd turned off the interstate.

"Pitman arm," the man repeated. Walter wondered if he could say anything else.

"What's it going to take to fix it?" Aunt Edie asked.

Gigi, at least that's what the name tag on the girl's shirt said, turned to her father.

"Three days."

"What? We don't have three days," Aunt Edie croaked.

"Rare part."

Walter was seriously beginning to wonder if the man could say more than two words at a time.

"Can we rush the part?" Gigi asked.

He nodded. "It'll cost."

Aunt Edie waved her hands wildly. "We've got to get back on

the road tomorrow afternoon at the latest. FedEx it, if you have to."

Gigi looked to her father and back to Aunt Edie. "We could rush the job, but that would cost you extra, since it would put us behind on our other projects."

"I'll pay it," Aunt Edie said.

Walter couldn't believe what he was hearing. Uncle Jerome used to complain that Aunt Edie would pinch a penny until Lincoln hollered, but ever since they'd started this trip Aunt Edie had been acting as though money were no object.

Or as though she wasn't going to need her portion.

"Look, those ashes belong to my husband, and I promised him that I would scatter them in several particular locations, including Neyland Stadium," Aunt Edie was saying.

"Well, considering the way they're playing this year, who knows if there'll be a season next year," Gigi said drily. "We'll be sure to get you back on the road by tomorrow."

Aunt Edie nodded with such a solemn expression that Walter couldn't help but chuckle, even though he tried to disguise it as a cough. The whole thing was beyond weird: spreading ashes, an orange-and-white hearse, and planning things around a college football game.

Aunt Edie worked things out with the mechanics, and they took all of their luggage out of the Caddy. Grandma Janice had the biggest suitcase. Peyton only had a backpack, but she wouldn't touch the cookie jar so Walter pulled his case behind him and cradled the cookie jar against his chest.

By the way Grandma Janice walked as they crossed the gravel parking lot to get to the shady-looking motel, Walter guessed she still hadn't reconciled herself to the gas station bathroom. She danced as they stood at the registration desk, reminding him of his potty-training nephew.

"Would you just go to the bathroom already?" Aunt Edie hissed. She nodded in the direction of a tiny bathroom in the lobby. She turned to the hotel clerk. "Could we please get a couple of rooms for the night?"

The clerk, a portly woman with stringy black hair, laughed. "Lady, you could book the whole hotel if you wanted to."

"Be that as it may, I think two rooms will do. Adjoining, please."

Walter looked at Peyton, who looked back at him then blushed. He hadn't thought of the sleeping arrangements, but he supposed it would be extravagant for them to get three or four rooms. Now faced with the idea of sleeping near so many strangers, he was extra-glad he'd packed his basketball shorts. He wondered if he would get one of those rooms all to himself. The last thing his mother had said to him was, "You keep your eye on that girl. Stay away from her."

Grandma Janice returned from the restroom exuding relief. "Did you ask about any discounts?"

"Discounts?" both Edie and the clerk said in unison.

"Triple A? AARP? Harvey always said those things would get us a discount."

"The rooms are a flat rate of seventy dollars each. It's all we've got, and it's all you'll find in Bucksnort. Let me tell you that."

Undaunted, Grandma Janice took her wallet from her purse. "At least let me pay," she said as she extended her American Express.

"Ma'am, we don't take that. Cash only."

Walter's eyes bugged out. What kind of place *was* this? He'd seen the adult store between the motel and the gas station. He was definitely *not* going to be telling his mother about this part of the trip. She'd never let him out of the house again.

Aunt Edie handed over several crisp twenties as though she were a veteran of seedy hotels. Grandma Janice had taken a step behind, her face flush with embarrassment. Finally, she spoke, "I have cash."

"I'll handle it," Aunt Edie said. "He was my husband and it's my responsibility."

With the arrangements made, they all headed outside to find their rooms on the side of the motel away from the interstate.

"Wait a minute, Edie. Why do we only have two keys?" Grandma Janice asked.

"Because we only have two rooms."

Walter felt a sudden urge to go for a run, to get far away before the fireworks started.

5

"What do you mean we only have two rooms?" Janice asked. She could not believe her sister-in-law. Did the woman have no sense? She wasn't sharing a bed with Edie, she was sure Peyton didn't want to share a bed with an old lady, and clearly Walter needed a room all to himself. Three rooms. She didn't have to go to college to be able to do that kind of math.

"Look, they are charging an obscene amount of money for these rooms. I am *not* paying for a third." Edie fumbled with the lock to the point that Peyton finally took the key card from her and slid it in gently until it agreed to let them enter. She handed the other key card to the kids and nodded to the room next door.

"This isn't the time to scrimp," Janice said.

"Actually, it *is* the time to scrimp because we don't know what it will cost to fix the rust bucket that brought us here," Edie said.

Janice surveyed the run-down interior and clutched her purse to her chest. She had never stayed in a hotel before. Never really thought about it, either. Maybe it would be good to keep everyone closer, but, boy, did it chap her hide that Edie could be all *"money is no object"* one moment and *"let's only get two rooms"* the next, as if propriety wasn't something to consider. Then again, maybe Edie was right; they would need any money that was leftover to fight off whatever communicable diseases they picked up in this motel.

Or bedbugs. Dear God, they had better not have bedbugs.

Her hands shook as she took out her new smart phone in an effort to check the bedbug registry her friend Louise had told her about.

No bars.

She'd have to ask one of the kids to look it up for her later. She looked at the connecting door and whispered, "I don't understand why we have enough money for the car, but not enough money for three rooms."

"I don't mind spending money," Edie hissed back, "but, one, there's no telling what the repairs will cost, and two, I'm not rewarding accommodations like this. That would be negative reinforcement."

Janice rolled her eyes. More teacher speak. What in the dickens did "negative reinforcement" even mean?

"You know what, Janice? I know you don't like me, and I can assure you the feeling has almost always been mutual, but do you think we could at least try to get along for one weekend? Believe it or not, I did love him as much, if not more, than you did."

Almost always mutual? There was a time when Edie hadn't hated her? Not that she could remember.

Edie unlocked the connecting door, and the kids' chatter spilled in from the other side. Hoping they wouldn't hear her, she whispered, "Look, I tried to like you. Really, I did. But you've made it pretty impossible."

Edie crossed her arms and leaned back to give Janice the

arched eyebrow she'd no doubt used to keep her high school students in line. "Funny. I could say the same about you."

***

Edie thought about kicking Janice in the back of one knee just to watch her fall down. It would be glorious. Maybe she'd also be able to give the woman some varicose veins, since it was hardly fair that she, the avid walker, had spidery veins all around her legs while Janice had the legs of a fifty-year-old. No, they could pass for forty-year-old legs, still firm and vein-free.

About that time Peyton dashed in from the adjoining room and cannonballed onto one of the beds.

"Don't sit on the bedspread!" Janice shrieked. "Haven't you watched *Dateline*? Don't you know what people *do* in these places? And they never wash the spread. No, they certainly do not."

Well, this is going to be a fun trip.

Peyton hopped off the bed, and Janice pulled the spread down, folding it over itself until only a little remained at the foot of the bed. "There. Now, Peyton, would you prefer to sleep with Edie or with me?"

"I don't see why I have to share a bed with anyone," Peyton said. "There are four beds and four of us. You can keep the door between the rooms open."

"Peyton, dear. It wouldn't be proper for you to spend the night in the same room as Walter."

"Oh, come off it," Edie heard herself saying. "The girl is right. We can just leave the door open."

Janice gasped. She would've clutched a necklace of pearls if she'd been wearing any, and honestly, Edie was surprised that she wasn't. "Edie, you cannot be serious."

"As a heart attack. It's 2011. We are right here, and these are two trustworthy teenagers. There's no need to subject that child to my snoring."

"In that case, I will march down there and get another room."

Truly, the woman was impossible.

"This particular cause doesn't need a martyr. The kids will be fine."

Janice stepped to within a foot of her. She was able to look down only because she was wearing those ridiculous heels. "We have an obligation to Peyton's parents."

"As if they care," Peyton said. She slipped past them into the other room. Janice's nostrils flared, but she didn't call the girl back.

"Grandma, do you have some toothpaste I could borrow later? I forgot mine." Walter stood in the adjoining doorway, taking up most of the space.

"Yes, I—" Janice started before she saw Walter was standing there barefoot.

"Put on your shoes!" she said. "The germs on this floor alone!"

Edie had had enough.

"Janice, get on your side of the door and leave those kids alone or I will shut the door tonight so they won't have to listen to your paranoid ramblings."

"Edie, I am just trying to keep everyone healthy and safe and—"

"As your brother always said, you gotta eat a peck of dirt before you die. Consider it a workout for their immune systems. Now, come in here and try to relax or I will go down to the bar and find some whiskey to help you out."

Janice, a teetotaler, gasped as Edie had known she would. "You wouldn't go down there by yourself, would you?"

"I may go anyway. You're running my blood pressure up.

Besides, we all need a good night's sleep so we can get up early in the morning and be ready to go by six thirty."

"Six thirty?" Peyton and Walter said together in that whiny voice teenagers wielded so well.

"Up and at 'em by six thirty. Just in case the car's ready."

"Just in case? Oh, put a sock in it!" Janice said. "The Grand Ole Opry box office probably doesn't open until ten, and there's no way the car will be ready by then. They probably don't even have the part in yet. Who knows if the car will even be safe once they fix it? We should just go home and forget about the whole thing. What does any of this matter to Jerome anyway?"

Edie did a double take. Was that a hint of moisture in Janice's eyes? Was she aware of the fact that waterproof mascara wasn't really waterproof?

"Now, Janice. I know you love your beauty rest and that hotel rooms are obviously trying for you, but—"

"I wouldn't know. This is the first time I've ever stayed in one."

That gave Edie pause. She felt something akin to pity that Janice had never been anywhere before. At least Jerome had been willing to go pretty much anywhere he could drive. No wonder her sister-in-law was so scared of the world. "Tell you what. We'll get up at seven and take it from there, how about that?"

Sounds of muffled celebration came from next door.

Janice sniffed.

Edie continued, "I'll ask Gigi to look the car over before we drive it, too."

"Like we can trust this Gigi person and that man she was with. He can't say more than three words at a time."

"Two, actually."

"Two? Three? Does it matter?"

The kids peeked through the door to see who would win the

battle of wills. Edie rolled her shoulders back. She was going to win, and everyone was going to like it.

But did it really matter?

"You're right," she heard herself say.

She'd never really thought about Janice's lack of travel experience before, but now she wondered whether her sister-in-law had ever wandered more than a county or two away from Yessum. She sincerely doubted it.

"Eight," Janice said, pouncing on Edie's moment of hesitation. "I think eight will be plenty early."

Edie nodded and let her have that small hour-long victory. "All right, kids, nothing to see here." She reached into her oversized purse and pulled out a couple of mystery novels. "Why don't you go read a book or something?"

6

*R*ead? Peyton was all about reading, but not on a crisp fall day after she'd been cooped up in a car, practically hyperventilating because it was a hearse. After assuring her chaperones that she would be safe outside in the large grassy area that was probably intended for semi parking, Peyton put a soccer ball under one arm and a football under the other and motioned for Walter to join her outside. He put down the book he'd been reading, *Life of Pi*, and joined her.

For a while they played soccer, dribbling the ball up and down the field, actively trying to steal the ball from one another. Walter had more power and athleticism, but Peyton was sneakier and soon had more steals. She also soon had him panting because her endurance outpaced his power and speed.

"Peyton, man, I gotta stop. You're killing me," he finally said.

She juggled the ball from foot to foot.

"I had no idea you were this good," Walter said.

"That's because no one goes to our games," she said.

"Well, I'm going to watch you play at least once this spring," he said.

Did her heart give an extra little beat? What was that about?

"Thank you."

"What about some football, now that you've handed my as—butt to me in soccer?"

"Sure."

Peyton jogged over to the side of the field where she'd left the football.

"Go long," she shouted.

Walter jogged down the field, but her throw was far too short. He picked up the ball and threw it to her, a perfect spiral that she caught with a grunt.

"I'm sorry, Peyton!"

"For what? That was an awesome pass. Do it again." She tossed him the ball, then ran down the field. They played this way for some time. She only caught one pass of his next six, but she was still laughing. That sixth ball got away from her and bounced almost toward the gravel. Peyton thought about throwing it, but her arms were tired. Instead she ran past the ball, then turned around to kick it.

It was an awful kick for a football. She didn't know form and she had no tee, but the ball went quite far in spite of these disadvantages, and Walter looked at her, hand on his hips. "Where'd you learn to do that?"

She jogged to meet him. "I don't know. I watch football, and I'm always the one in charge of penalty kicks on our team."

"They could use you next year," Walter said. "I'm graduating, and they don't have anyone who can kick."

She licked her chapped lips. "Wanna teach me?"

They worked the rest of the afternoon until Peyton knew that her face and the back of her neck were sunburned. Walter taught her how to kick for an extra point and showed her the basics of punting. She was far better at the former than the latter, but even she could tell she would be a good punter with practice. Finally, the offending sun slid behind the seedy-looking motel.

"Why haven't you ever tried out for the football team?" Walter asked as they walked back to the motel.

She shrugged. "They don't exactly send out gold-engraved invitations to the girls."

"Maybe they should."

"Well, maybe I'll ask."

"You do that."

She grinned at his insistence. She'd never thought about playing football, but maybe he was right.

"My mom was actively against me playing football," he admitted.

"That why you're a kicker?" Peyton asked.

Walter bristled. "What's wrong with being a kicker?"

Peyton hesitated. "Nothing, but with your height and that arm, you could be a quarterback."

He snorted. "If there's nothing wrong with being a kicker, why'd you pause?"

"Well, you get to put on the pads and go out there, but it's not like being a *real* football player."

"A *real* football player?"

Peyton's heart hammered. She'd made a mistake. "I mean, it's not like you're out there all the time. I'd be a kicker. If they'd let me."

"Not out there all the time," Walter muttered as they reached the door to Miss Edie and Miss Janice's room. "'Not out there all the time'? Look, I go to the same practices and run the same drills. I lift weights and run laps and do all of the jumping jacks and push-ups, but I guess I'm not a *real* football player. Never mind the fact that three times this year I've been the one to tackle the jackass who returned my punts because those other boys couldn't stop him. Made one of 'em cry, I hit him so hard. But that's okay. I'm not a *real* football player."

Peyton opened her mouth to apologize, but Miss Edie opened the door before she could speak. "You're just in time. I ordered a pizza, and Janice is struggling to eat it because there are no knives or forks."

Walter pushed past the older lady, and Peyton considered running away rather than coming inside. Miss Edie cocked her head to one side and studied her, though, so she entered the room before the older lady could ask any questions.

***

Later, Peyton lay in bed, unable to go to sleep. Despite her big talk, it was the first time she'd ever shared a bedroom with a boy her age, and it was weird. Also, she was still thinking about what Walter had said about how she could be a kicker. She wanted to ask him more, but the door was open, and there was no telling what Miss Edie or Miss Janice would do if she and Walter tried to have a discussion. And third, she was afraid she would oversleep the next morning. Or sleepwalk. Or talk in her sleep.

In fact, she'd actually wanted a bed to herself because she'd been known to walk and talk in her sleep. She'd also been known to kick and punch. That had been happening ever since her uncle Hugh had sneaked into her bedroom a few years ago. Her cousins had warned her that he was handsy, but she didn't think he had the stones to come into her bedroom.

Unfortunately for him, she'd kneed him in the groin, causing the whole house to wake up and ensuring that Uncle Hugh was banned from the trailer from that point forward. As her daddy had said, *"I'm not much of a father, but I'm not letting any of that mess go on in my house."*

She shivered at the memory and got up to check the locks. She fingered the chain and tested the dead bolt. One of the ladies next door, Peyton couldn't tell which, had begun to snore. Then the other joined her, their snores playing off of each other like a weird nasal version of that "Dueling Banjos" song that Mr.

Jerome had liked so much. Every once in a while, he'd play that song with her daddy, since he was a fiddle player, too. For the longest time, she'd thought the song was called "Dueling Fiddles," until one day Mr. Jerome had laughed and explained to her that it was supposed to be banjos, but neither he nor her daddy knew how to play those.

She'd liked it when Mr. Jerome and Daddy used to play together, but she really, really liked "Orange Blossom Special." Even as an old man, Mr. Jerome had been able to play the fast and light notes of the song. Her eyes would glaze over as she watched his bow move over the strings, and her foot would tap so fast that her ankle ached. He'd told her how some bluegrass bands would make any potential fiddle player prove his worth by playing that song and how it was the fiddle player's anthem.

Sometimes the University of Tennessee band would play "Orange Blossom Special," so it had become associated with two of his favorite things: fiddles and football. That had to be why he'd named the hearse after the tune. Now Mr. Jerome had rewarded her with something she didn't deserve and hadn't been able to imagine—a chance for a college education—and she'd gone and mucked up all of those good feelings by insulting Walter. Mr. Jerome wouldn't have stood for that; he was kind to everyone.

"Walter?" she whispered, even though she was beginning to think a freight train going through the connecting door wouldn't wake up either of the women in the other room. "Are you awake?"

"I don't see how anyone in a five-mile radius is asleep."

"I'm really sorry for what I said earlier. You're a real football player. In fact, you're a real good one. I bet you could play any position you wanted to."

The snores rose and fell next door. Peyton had given up hope he would answer her, but he finally spoke. "That's all right. It just really cut me because that's the way my cousins talk. They know Mama wouldn't let me play any other position and they tease me about it all the time."

"Why won't she?"

"She's read all that stuff about concussions, and she watches the way some ballplayers waste their money. She makes me read every story she can find about a football player who squandered his money and now works as a janitor somewhere because he didn't finish his college degree. She doesn't want that kind of life for me. I finally got her to see that I needed to at least *try* for an athletic scholarship, or she'd never be able to help my brothers and sister all get through college. She's already broke with one of us in college, and there are two more behind me."

Peyton thought about it for a minute. She hadn't given much thought to concussions or injury, although she'd watched enough games and seen players being taken out on a stretcher. She couldn't imagine her parents telling her no for any of those reasons, though. If she could make money, but only at the risk of injury, her parents would be all about her taking the risk for the chance at some cash.

"Well, I'm sorry. And I think you're a good son for listening to her and that you're lucky to have a mother who cares that much about you. You're a good punter and a really good kicker."

"Thank you."

He seemed okay with her, but she couldn't see his eyes in the dark.

"Wait. You don't have to play football at all with this scholarship from Mr. Jerome."

"Yeah, but if I get a scholarship, then I can give what money we've saved back to Mama to help with my brothers. Besides, now I don't have to go to Jefferson State. I can try to walk on at UT, maybe see if they'll let me play another position."

"Well, we'll ask Mr. Little if they can have my money, too," Peyton said in a small voice.

"What do you mean? You gotta go to school with that money. No one else can have it."

"Nah. My ACT scores are too low. I'm too stupid for college."

"That's ridiculous. Don't I see you reading books all the time?"

"Oh, the reading part's fine, but I'm behind in math. They keep putting me in the dummy class, and we hardly get past addition and multiplication."

They lay in silence, and Peyton surprised herself by yawning. Even without the comforter, she was getting toasty under the ratty blanket, and the snores next door were fading.

"I can help you with math," Walter said softly. "If Uncle Jerome wanted you to go to college, you should go. He wouldn't have suggested it if he didn't think you could do it."

Peyton felt warmth radiate from the inside out. Not only did Walter think she was smart enough for college, but he was willing to help her with her math. And her kicking! At the thought of studying with him, her hands got clammy, but she was excited, too.

She only wished she could ask Mr. Jerome why he'd thought she needed to go to college. She understood his gift to Walter because they were kin, but she'd never thought of herself as anything more than Mr. Jerome's football buddy.

"Hey, Peyton?"

Something about Walter's voice gave her a shivery feeling. "What?"

"You *are* smart, you know."

All of her warm and shivery feelings collided with one another. She wanted to study with him, and she wanted to run away before he could see exactly how bad her grades were. She finally went to sleep, fantasizing about what a kiss from Walter might be like, but it was a restless, uneasy sleep because her nerves continued to thrum.

7

The next morning Edie the Drill Sergeant roused her troops and ordered them through showers, packing, and vending machine Pop-Tarts in the lobby while they waited for Gigi to show. She told no one about the dread in the pit of her stomach that Gigi might take their Cadillac and their money but never show up. She'd memorized the license plate of the tow truck—just in case.

Edie ignored the grunts of her tripmates as morning stretched long. They didn't need as much sleep as they thought they did. She paced the tiny porch of the motel while Walter and Peyton tossed the football in the grassy space out front. The fresh air had to be good for them, even if they were drawing it in while playing in front of the Wanton Redneck's Love Shack. Blessedly, neither teen had asked about the establishment nor expressed interest in visiting.

Just as Edie was about to call the police, the tow truck turned into the gravel lot, followed by the Orange Blossom Special. Her heart actually skipped a beat at the sight of it, and she took the steps too quickly, twisting her ankle in the process.

Gigi met her in the drive. "Well, the Pitman arm had given

out, but we managed to replace it. I'm not sure we used the best part for the job, but it should take care of you until you can get back home. I also changed the oil, checked your tire pressure, and refilled your washer fluid. You've got a little bit of an oil leak, but you should be fine until you get back."

"Thank you. How much do I owe you?"

Gigi responded with a number that made Janice say a naughty word, as well as knock over the cookie jar, spilling a little bit of Jerome in the process. Edie gave her sister-in-law a dirty look, then turned back to the mechanic. "Will a check be okay?"

"Usually we don't take checks from out-of-towners."

"That's fine," Edie said. "I think I have my American Express right here."

"No good," said Gigi's father, who'd come to stand beside her.

"Okay." Edie dug through her pocketbook. "I think I have a Visa. How about that?"

Gigi took her phone from her pocket and attached a little square device before scanning the card. She presented Edie with a printout of everything they'd done, then held out a smaller receipt for her to sign. In less than five minutes, they'd shaken hands, and Edie had called for the kids to come load up the car.

She turned to see Janice trying to sweep Jerome back into the cookie jar. One of Carmen Miranda's grapes had broken off. "Oh, leave it."

"I can't leave him here!"

"Of course, you can. He'd get a kick out of the Wanton Redneck's Love Shack."

Janice gasped, giving Edie time to collect the cookie jar before she could sweep that tiny bit of Jerome along with a greater amount of dirt inside. She cradled Carmen Miranda under one arm and addressed kids and sister-in-law alike.

"Anyone need to pee before we get on the road? I'd like to make the Ryman before it closes."

"Do you have to be so vulgar, Edie?" Janice asked, but she did turn to reenter the motel.

Both Peyton and Walter refused to take advantage of the facilities. Peyton held out her hand for the keys, but Edie almost handed them to Walter instead. Then she thought about herself at that age. The kid hadn't caused the old boat to break. She needed to hop back on the horse. Edie dropped the keys into her outstretched hand.

"Fine, but I'm driving next." Walter said it with a smile, though, before loading up the luggage without being asked. They were such good kids. Why hadn't she seen them as Jerome had? Too many times in the past she'd seen them just as nuisances who dirtied the floor or ate all of the Oreos, but now she saw them as people—people who'd listened to all of Jerome's silly carryings-on. They hadn't known about his money when they watched football with him and asked questions, but he'd seen two good kids who were going to have trouble paying for a college education.

He'd made those kids his own.

Edie teared up a bit at lost opportunities. No doubt they would end this trip and run off to college and leave her alone, because she hadn't been as invested in them as Jerome had. She could've been. If she'd stopped what she was doing to watch the game with them, or maybe even had worked on her cross-stitch in the same room with them. Maybe then she would've created a similar bond.

No matter. She still had her bottle of pills, and everyone would be better off without her.

The kids were already in the front seat ready to go when Janice finally emerged from the motel lobby. "Why in heaven's name did you pay those people so much money to get this boat running?"

"It's my money, and I'll do with it as I please."

Janice opened her mouth either to protest or to complain more about the expense, but Edie cut her off. "No. Really. It's my money now. I paid as much into the household as Jerome did. Maybe I decided those two poor mechanics needed a little extra for plying their trade in Bucksnort. Maybe I have more money than sense. Or maybe I don't plan on needing that much money in the near future."

Before her companion could respond, Edie clutched Jerome to her chest and climbed into the car. It took Janice a little longer since she had to walk around to get in behind the driver's side, wobbling on her ridiculous pumps. Finally, she slid into the backseat of the hearse and smoothed her skirt before fastening her seat belt.

"Peyton, let's get this show on the road," she said brightly.

It was a show, all right.

More like a clown car of death.

When Janice dug through her pocketbook for her compact, Edie couldn't take it any longer. "You do know the funeral is over, so you don't have to keep dressing up, right?"

"What's it to you, sugar mama?" Janice asked as she reapplied her lipstick and patted her hair.

"It's ridiculous. There's more to life than appearance."

Janice stiffened, and Edie wondered if she'd gone too far.

After a heavy silence, Peyton squeaked, "How 'bout them Vols?"

"No, I think it's time we settled this once and for all." Janice snapped the compact shut and turned in her seat to face Edie. In the process of putting the compact back into her purse, she'd elbowed Carmen Miranda. Edie reached out to steady the jar.

"Not all of us got to go to school and get a fancy education," Janice said. "Some of us had to stay home and raise babies."

There it was again, Janice's second-favorite accusation: that she was selfish. "That has nothing to do with why anyone would voluntarily wear control-top panty hose and high heels on a five-hour drive."

"Oh, I forgot," Janice added acerbically. "Not all of us can be ridiculously thin our whole lives. Of course, not having children helped you with that."

"Oh yes. You've discovered my secret at long last: I've avoided control top panty hose by not having children."

"So. Think we can turn things around after that awful Arkansas game?" Peyton asked, obviously trying again.

"I thought we weren't talking about football," Walter said.

"But it would be a shame not to talk about how we mopped the floor with Middle Tennessee the week before," Peyton said through clenched teeth, nodding at the backseat.

This time Walter caught on. "Oh. Yeah. Now, *that* game was a thing of beauty. Do you think we'll finally have Bray back for the game tomorrow?"

"You know, I was just reading about that—"

"Oh, come off it, you two," Edie said. It came out harsher than she'd intended, and she was actually grateful they had intervened. They were such sweet kids. She tried again, this time calmer, nicer. "Know what? I think some real food would improve our dispositions. I see a Waffle House ahead. Why don't we stop and get a proper breakfast?"

"At noon?" Janice snorted.

"Eat what you please, Janice."

Stopping for a few minutes would give Edie time to compose herself. Or maybe they could leave Janice behind in the bathroom "accidentally on purpose" when they left.

8

*J*anice told herself she wasn't going to feel guilty about what she'd said. She also told herself not to covet the eggs, hash browns, and waffles her companions were eating. So what if she had to eat oatmeal because it was the only healthy thing on the menu? At least she was finally getting some decent coffee. Come to think of it, she probably wouldn't have said the things she did if she'd had a half-decent cup of coffee. By the time Gigi and her Father of the Two-Word Phrases had pulled up, she'd had a caffeine withdrawal headache threatening to bloom into a migraine.

They finished their meal in silence, and Edie took the check. She turned to Janice with a smug smile and opened her mouth to speak, but Janice cut her off. "I'm going to the restroom right now, all right?"

She really hated it when Edie was so crass, always asking everyone whether or not they had to pee. Who did that? She'd had to cut Walter off in the middle of breakfast, too, because he'd wanted to talk about some football injury he'd witnessed. No one wanted to hear such things while they were eating.

Janice did her business and washed her hands, turning her

face left and right as she looked into the mirror. Harvey had told her constantly that she was still beautiful, but all of those wrinkles had snuck up on her and no amount of makeup in the world could cover them up. Edie was one to talk about not being dressed up, since her clothes always hung so nicely. Even if Edie hadn't been rail-thin, she would've had her education to recommend her. If Janice wasn't dressed up, then what exactly did she have going for her? She didn't have an education. She didn't have a size-six body. She'd dutifully raised her children and sent them out into the world. She'd kept her house pristine —but now what was she supposed to do? She couldn't even "look good," now that she was old and saggy with the potbelly that had doggedly pursued her for her entire life.

Easy for Edie to think she was overdressed.

But Edie was right about one thing: Panty hose were *so* uncomfortable while sitting in a car for hours on end.

"Janice, you try too hard," Jerome had once said.

Coming from him, it had always seemed more concern than criticism.

He'd then added, *"You need to lighten up, take care of yourself more. I don't know why you women insist on shoving your legs into nylons like sausage into a casing. It's about as stupid as that line you used to draw down the back of your legs when you couldn't get any nylons back during the war."*

Well, Jerome, you never had a potbelly to worry about, now, did you?

And he would've said, *"Who're you trying to impress? It's my funeral. Let it all hang out!"*

So, Janice lifted her skirt and started to peel down the control-top hose. Once the waistband wasn't eating into the flesh of a belly that had so kindly borne her three children, she couldn't help but sigh in relief. "Know what, Jerome? I'm taking these off. Just for you."

She held on to the sink with one hand and unwrapped one

heel before gingerly switching sides. She made sure to put each foot carefully back into its shoe. No way were her bare feet going to so much as touch a nasty public restroom floor.

Then she dropped her hose.

"Oh no."

There was no turning back now. She picked up the hose between her thumb and forefinger and deposited them into the trash can. She washed her hands in the hottest water she could stand before bothering to smooth her skirt down. As she did so, she looked at her legs. They were a little pale, but they still looked pretty darn good if she did say so herself.

She took an extra paper towel to open the bathroom door, admittedly feeling freer, but she stopped short when she saw a couple of bearded guys sitting at the booth where her party had been. She looked back to the restroom, but no one waited for her in the narrow hallway.

It was silly for her stomach to drop. They couldn't have left without her. They wouldn't risk everyone's inheritance, and, more than that, it would be cruel. She walked outside, the chilly air nipping at her newly liberated legs.

The Orange Blossom Special was nowhere to be seen.

9

"*A*unt Edie, I don't think Grandma is going to find this funny at all."

"Go back around the corner, then," Edie said. "Your granny needs to learn to lighten up."

One look at Janice standing on the curb with her hands on her hips, and Edie wondered if she'd miscalculated.

"Walter Daniel Hines, that was *not* funny," Edie's nemesis said as she slipped into the backseat. Her ears were pink, and color bloomed across her cheeks. She appeared to be in a fit of righteous anger. "You are in big trouble, young man."

She brought one shaking hand up to point at him, but in the process, she knocked over the cookie jar with the pocketbook she had slung over her arm.

Carmen Miranda fell over, spilling a bit of Jerome on the floorboard. A bit of breeze floated his dust out to the Waffle House parking lot.

"Oh," Janice said, staring at the cookie jar.

"What's going on back there?" Walter asked.

"Just a little spill." Edie grunted as she picked up the cookie jar and placed the fruit hat back on Carmen Miranda. She knew she should've ignored Jerome's wishes and bought a real urn.

"Wait. A spill? Of Uncle Jerome?" Walter slammed on the brakes, and the cookie jar toppled onto the floorboard once again, spilling a few more of his ashes.

Edie could feel her heartbeat in her ears.

Then she laughed.

The other three people in the car looked at her as though they wondered whether the next stop should be the loony bin rather than the Ryman Auditorium, but Edie could only think about how amused Jerome would be. He'd make a joke about how he was sure enough going to have to get the old car detailed.

"What is wrong with you?" Janice asked, her voice so low that Edie could tell she was truly horrified and not just putting on her usual show.

"Jerome is wanting to participate in our journey, can't you see?"

"No, I do not see. It's a travesty, and we need to do something about the lid to that thing."

"I think it cracked back at the hotel," Edie said.

"We left some of Mr. Jerome back at that crappy motel?" Peyton asked.

"Yes, yes, we did." Edie giggled again.

"I don't know what's gotten into you." Janice narrowed her eyes. "Or Walter, either, for that matter."

"Don't blame the boy," Edie said as she wiped away a tear of laughter. "It was my idea to play a little joke on you because you spend so much time in the bathroom."

"I do not!"

"And I didn't think it would make you mad. Seemed like something Jerome would do."

Janice considered. "Yeah. It is something he would've done."

"I truly am sorry. I didn't mean to worry you. I hope you know I wouldn't actually strand you at a Waffle House."

"I guess not," Janice grumbled. Edie figured that was as close to a truce as she and Janice would get.

"Then the ashes spilled, and I thought about how much Jerome loved this damn car and his damn Waffle House and how it would serve him right to have to clean up this mess, but, of course, he *can't* clean up the mess. And the whole thing struck me as funny, because I was going to end up being the one to take the car to be cleaned out, and then what would I say? 'Please be sure to vacuum up my husband's ashes from the back of his orange-and-white hearse.'"

Peyton was the first to giggle.

Then Walter chuckled, despite a valiant effort to hold it in.

Already far from composed, Edie started laughing again, a distinctive wheezing sound that made the kids laugh all the harder. Finally, Janice succumbed. They all sat in a pothole-ridden parking lot and laughed until they cried.

Finally, Edie calmed down enough to give Walter directions, even though he told her his phone would get them all there just fine. Her stomach muscles ached from laughing. She looked over to Janice to see how mad she was, but something was different.

"Janice, what did you do with your panty hose?"

"I no longer wished for my top to be controlled, so I took them off."

Well. Okay, then.

***

Finally, Edie told Walter they'd pay for two spaces to accommodate the hearse.

He had tried three times to fit the car into a single parking spot, but eventually pulled smack-dab into the middle of two spaces, and Edie couldn't blame him. Who knew where they were going to park the thing when they got to Knoxville? It had been a long time since she'd returned to her alma mater, but she doubted that parking had gotten any easier there.

Edie looked at the complicated machine in the middle of the parking lot. She'd been expecting to just slide cash into the appropriate slots, but the world kept changing.

"Do you know your PIN, Miss Edie?" Peyton asked.

"Of course, I know my PIN." *I think.* "But I would rather pay cash."

"I don't think that's an option."

"Apparently not." Edie passed Carmen Miranda over to Peyton, who held the jar at arm's length as though it might bite her, and fished through her purse for her debit card. Walter read the numbers on the screen for her, and she got their parking squared away even if cash would've been a heckuva lot easier for *her*. She took the cookie jar from Peyton and started power walking across the lot.

"What in heaven's name are you doing?" Janice asked.

"I'm taking Jerome to the home of the Grand Ole Opry. What does it look like I'm doing?"

"Do you really think they're going to let you waltz in there and scatter his ashes all over the place?"

Janice had a point, but Edie didn't want to concede it. "Maybe I'll tell them it's the 'Tennessee Waltz.'"

Peyton snickered. Walter coughed into his arm, but it sounded suspicious as coughs went.

"Seriously. Why not scoop out a little into something else? We've already spilled him in three other places."

"And just where do you propose we put the little bit of him that we scoop out?"

Janice opened her mouth then closed it before turning to her pocketbook, a bag so big she could practically stick her head inside. She emerged with an economy-size ibuprofen bottle. "How about this?"

"What are you going to do with the pills?"

She drew out another bottle. "I have two bottles. I meant to transfer the older pills in with the new, but I got distracted with packing."

Yes. That makes sense.

The whole thing was so ridiculous. If she'd had any idea what this trip was going to be like, she would've put her request in to the good Lord to pass away first, but nooooo, she'd been oh-so-concerned about how Jerome would take care of himself if she were gone. Now she was about to pour ashes from a ridiculously cheerful cookie jar into an economy-size ibuprofen bottle in order to spread her husband's remains in a historic building. On the sly.

And *that* sounded like something that would happen in a macabre Dr. Seuss book.

Wait a minute. In what part of the will did it say that *she* had to do the spreading? "That's a great idea you have there. Why don't you do the pouring and spreading?"

"I believe I will." Janice handed Carmen Miranda's fruit hat to Peyton and motioned for Walter to hold the ibuprofen bottle. She pursed her lips as she gently tipped the bottom half of the jar to pour some ashes into the bottle. "I'm so sorry, Jerome, but I don't know of a better way."

"I really don't think he minds at this point," Edie said. "He's probably laughing at us right now."

Janice managed to get the lid back on the cookie jar and handed it over to Edie. "If I'm doing the pouring, then you can walk him back to the car."

When Edie rejoined her companions, Peyton had shielded her eyes from the sun and was studying the Ryman. "I don't see anything about football here, and that building looks like a church. Why are we here?"

10

"Didn't you ever hear Jerome play the fiddle?" Janice asked as they all walked around the building to find the entrance.

"Yeah, but what does that have to do with a church?" Peyton asked.

"This is the home of the Grand Ole Opry. Jerome used to listen to the radio programs and then pick out the songs on his fiddle."

"Oh! This is where he learned about 'Dueling Fid—Banjos'?"

Janice chuckled. "Nah, he picked that one up quickly. My brother was a really, really good fiddle player, you know. Before he went off to the war, he was in a group that played all around the Southeast, but he had to give that up."

"What happened?" Peyton asked as they reached the lobby. Edie went to pay for tickets, and Janice decided to let her.

"He got drafted."

"Why didn't he go back to playing the fiddle when he got home?" Peyton persisted. Janice noticed that Walter was listening to the story, too.

"A couple of reasons," she said. "He'd injured himself in the

Pacific, and he wasn't as good as he'd been before. He was out of practice, too. Mostly, though, he didn't feel like playing. Then there was the fact that Mama and Daddy wanted him to take advantage of the G.I. Bill and go to college because neither of them had ever made it past the eighth grade."

"Wow."

Wow, indeed. Janice didn't have the heart to tell Peyton that she'd never made it past tenth grade herself. She'd married Harvey, and that was that. She didn't have a high school diploma to her name despite being the one who kept the family farm afloat while Jerome was gone. She'd even worked in the munitions plant up in Hightown for part of the war, sometimes putting in forty- and fifty-hour weeks in addition to keeping the cows fed and milked.

"Anyway, at some point after he got back from the war, Jerome heard 'Orange Blossom Special' on the radio, and that was a song he really wanted to play. He finally got his fiddle out of the closet and started practicing again. It took him hours to learn that song."

Peyton grinned. "I like it a lot."

At that point, the tour guide stepped up, so the four of them listened quietly to the history of the Ryman, how it had started as a tabernacle but ended up a shrine to country music. While they were on the balcony, however, Janice reached for the bottle. She would need to be stealthy. She would need to open the bottle while it was still in her purse.

Opening childproof bottles was a challenge now, thanks to arthritic knuckles, but she could do it. She would do it for Jerome. The tour guide gestured toward the stage, and everyone's eyes followed. They were about to leave. This was her chance.

Carefully, she lifted the bottle. The minute the tour guide turned her back, Janice dumped the bottle.

And two-hundred-and-fifty-plus tablets hit the floor with a clatter.

Dear God, she'd opened the wrong bottle.

Everyone turned to see what had happened, but it was her three companions who looked on in openmouthed horror.

"Um, I was getting a headache, and I accidentally spilled my Advil," Janice explained.

Walter and Peyton leaped into action, crouching down to pick up as many pills as they could. Edie's eyes narrowed. Of course, Edie would never do something so *stupid*.

"Leave it," said the tour guide. "I'll send someone up in a few minutes to sweep it up."

Walter and Peyton froze, but after checking with Janice they stood and followed the group downstairs.

Think, Janice, think!

She couldn't spread the ashes now, not knowing whether or not they would be swept up before they had a chance to become a part of the theater. She didn't know how much longer the tour would last, but she had to think of something.

Down they went into the theater proper, and Janice couldn't see a way out of the situation. She sidled up to Edie and whispered into her good ear, "I think you need to do it."

Edie threw up both hands. "Oh no. You didn't like the way I was doing things, so you can do it yourself."

Janice gritted her teeth as they made their way over to the stage. Where could she put the ashes? If she put them on the stage, they'd see her—and the ashes—for sure. It'd be disrespectful to put them in a trash can. She eyed the grand piano that was already onstage for a future performance. Did she dare?

The group followed the guide, but Janice lagged behind, pretending to study the stained-glass windows. Everyone got to step up onstage, but Janice lollygagged some more. She could really use some help, but she knew better than to ask Edie, and the kids were too busy taking selfies to pay attention to what she was doing. She would have to do this herself.

Carefully, she eased up the lid to the piano as much as she dared, just wide enough for the mouth of the bottle. She poured Jerome's ashes into the piano and was satisfied she was being stealthy—right up to the moment when the lid slammed down and everyone looked at her.

She drew the bottle behind her back. "I, ah, I've never seen inside one of these before," she said, her face burning hot.

"Ma'am, what are you doing?" the tour guide asked as she walked toward Janice.

Oh God. Please don't lift the lid. Please don't lift the lid. Please don't—

Edie grabbed the tour guide's arm. "Could you tell me more about the stained-glass windows? And didn't Tennessee Ernie Ford once sing here?"

The tour guide glared at Janice but apparently decided she wasn't a danger, so she turned to answer Edie's questions instead.

Janice wanted to wilt with relief against the piano, but she forced herself to slowly step toward the edge of the stage and shield her gaze with a trembling hand to look out into an imaginary audience. She could only hope her bumbling tourist impression would last until the tour guide forgot about her piano shenanigans.

Out of the corner of her eye, she saw Edie peppering the guide with one question after another. She'd never known Edie to have that much interest in the Opry, so she could only conclude that her nemesis had decided to help her at the last minute. For a bare second, she couldn't help but feel gratitude for Edie's quick thinking.

Finally, their beleaguered tour guide shooed the group toward the inevitable end of the tour: the gift shop.

Walter rubbed his stomach as they bypassed the shop and

headed back outdoors. "I'm hungry. Can we stop at the café over there?"

"No!" Edie and Janice said in unison.

"In fact, I think we need to get on the road if we're going to make it to Knoxville before it's dark," Edie said, clutching Walter's arm and then Peyton's. "So, let's get to stepping."

They walked so quickly that Janice was out of breath by the time they reached the car. Edie leaned against the hearse and gave that wheezing laugh of hers. "I have to hand it to you, Janice. I didn't realize what you were doing at first, but pretending to be clumsy was a stroke of genius."

Pretending? And had Edie Malcolm really just called *her* a genius? "Um, thank you."

"I mean, I didn't think you had it in you."

"Had what?" Peyton asked. "Did you manage to spread the ashes?"

"They're in the piano," Janice blurted.

"The piano?" Walter echoed. His stomach growled, and Janice felt a twinge of guilt about taking him away from the café. But only a twinge.

"Jerome is going to puff up out of the piano the minute someone starts to play," Edie said, sputtering as she laughed.

Janice stood up straighter. She should probably admit to Edie that the whole thing had been a lucky mistake, but she couldn't. The victory was too sweet.

"Ma'am? Ma'am?" Their tour guide ran toward them, and all four of them panicked and jumped into the hearse. Tires squealed as they pulled out of the parking lot. Only as they rolled past did Janice catch a glimpse of something white in an outstretched hand. Their tour guide had only been trying to return the bottle they left behind, the one that contained what was left of the ibuprofen.

11

"*A*re you sure they're not going to come after us?" Peyton asked for the third time.

Edie chuckled. "I'm sure."

"I didn't like that at all," Peyton said, hugging herself. She hadn't even wanted to drive when they'd stopped in Cookeville to stretch their legs and get something for Walter's growling stomach.

"It's okay. We shouldn't have any trouble with the next stop. Who could possibly care if we put ashes on a grave?"

"Cemeteries creep me out," Walter said.

"What about the stadium, though?" Peyton asked.

Persistent, that child.

But she was right about one thing: The stadium would be a challenge. It would take some kind of miracle for them to be able to get out onto the field and deposit what was left of Jerome in the end zone. Well, maybe not *all* that was left, because there was no way they'd be able to get the cookie jar through the gate.

We'll cross that bridge when we get there.

For now, there were more important questions to be

answered. "Louis' or Litton's?"

"What?" Janice and the kids asked together.

"Are we going to eat at Louis' or Litton's? This is the ultimate question."

"Wherever I can get the most food," Walter said.

"Hmmm, probably Louis', then. The spaghetti," Edie said.

"You just ate," said Janice. "Do you have a hollow leg or something?"

"Yeah. A hollow leg I want to fill with spaghetti."

And so he did. They all stuffed themselves silly, and Edie thought back to the time when she and Jerome had first discovered Louis' Restaurant. They'd been in town for a homecoming game and had ventured out to the north of town to see what all the fuss was about. Even now, she'd never had spaghetti sauce quite like Louis'. Did they put Parmesan in the sauce? Some kind of pepper?

"I've never eaten spaghetti in a restaurant," Peyton said. "So much better than the school cafeteria, too."

Edie studied the girl until she blushed. "Don't expect all restaurants to be this good. They're not, I'm afraid."

"I know that's the truth," Walter said as he leaned back and rubbed his taut belly. "Thank you for lunch, Aunt Edie."

"Yes, thank you," Peyton said.

"Maybe I should get this one," Janice said.

"Look, Jerome is paying for this meal since he has us gallivanting all over creation and doing things that aren't strictly legal. Lord knows, he left me more money than I'm ever going to need."

"Well, thank you," Janice said.

It was a begrudging thanks, but Edie paused, because she didn't think she'd ever heard her sister-in-law thank her for anything before.

***

After spending the night in a much nicer hotel than the one in Bucksnort, the merry band of ash spreaders, minus Janice, donned their orange. They ate an early breakfast at a Cracker Barrel and went in search of the general's grave.

They had to drive into town and past the Salvation Army mission and past Old Gray Cemetery. Down a side street they went, until they came to a military cemetery, one with uniform graves all in a row.

"Fitting for a general," Edie muttered. She got out at the little station that held information on how to find a certain grave, then directed Walter to drive around the cemetery until they had circled almost back to the entrance.

His marker stood amidst others, unpretentious, despite his place in Tennessee football lore. Edie carried Carmen Miranda this time, and they waited for a trio of Vols fans to leave before they all gathered around the general's final resting place.

"I never knew Uncle Jerome was so weird," Walter said as he looked over his shoulder for any potential ghosts. "First that church theater place, and now this?"

"I know they named the stadium after him, but what is the big deal about this guy?" Peyton asked.

Walter's eyes looked ready to pop out of his head. "The big deal is that General Neyland is the winningest coach in Tennessee history. He won four national championships, five SEC championships, and he had a bunch of undefeated seasons. There was one year when *no one* scored—not even once— against the Vols."

"Whoa."

"Damn straight, whoa."

"Walter, dear, please watch your language," Janice said, even though she seemed preoccupied by the cemetery herself.

Edie had to admit she hadn't known all of that about the general. Mainly, Jerome had liked to shout "Oskie!" a lot, and she knew the general had something to do with that nonsense.

Walter was on a mission to educate her, though. "He's got all of these maxims that football programs all over the nation still use today. He's a big deal."

"Do you think we ought to say a few words before we let Mr. Jerome commune with him?" Peyton asked.

Edie snorted. "What else is there to say? I think Jerome is hoping to meet the general in the great beyond and somehow convince him to send some mojo down to this year's squad."

Janice gave her a withering glance.

"Fine, we can sing a bar or two of 'Rocky Top.'"

"Please, no."

"What about the 'Tennessee Waltz'?" Walter asked. "The band plays it at the end of every home game."

"Fine." Edie took a deep, shaky breath, as she thought of her and Jerome's secret kitchen waltzes. "'I was waltzing—'"

"I don't remember the words," Peyton admitted.

"We can hum it, then," Janice suggested.

So, the odd foursome hummed the "Tennessee Waltz," then Edie poured another bit of Jerome over the general's grave.

"Time to go," Edie said as she closed the cookie jar. Janice gave her a dirty look for being so abrupt, but Edie turned on her heel anyway and walked off because she wasn't a fan of standing around in graveyards. She'd done enough of that already in her lifetime.

Yeah, and you're thinking about making others do it for you next.

Maybe she should hold off on her pill plan. Maybe she should make sure she'd made proper arrangements with the Andersons for her to be cremated. Unlike her ridiculous husband, though, she could just be unceremoniously dumped. They could throw her ashes in with the used oil over at Burger Paradise for all she cared.

But before she went, maybe she should make a stop of her own. If Jerome could make all of these crazy requests, then she had to be entitled to at least one memory of her own.

---

*T*ruth be told, Edie was mad that Jerome's final wishes revolved around a bunch of things she didn't like and a bunch of places he'd never taken her. She didn't play the fiddle, and he rarely played for her. She cared very little for football—other than her fervent wish that Tennessee might always beat Alabama and the occasional Dallas Cowboys game —and, even so, she should probably look into a new hobby, based on how well that had been going the past few years.

Since Jerome hadn't thought of places they'd visited together, she would do the thinking for him. She directed Walter to drive back into town. It took them a few minutes, but they finally managed to maneuver the Orange Blossom Special into a parking garage somewhere behind Gay Street.

Edie looked up at the old S&W Café. Her heart had momentarily leapt into her throat, because she thought the grand old cafeteria was still open, but it wasn't. She'd missed its grand reopening and then its quiet closing by only a year or so, if the sign on the door was to be believed. Even so, she remembered how fancy the cafeteria had seemed, how proud Jerome had been to take her to a "nice restaurant" for their first date.

They'd even had an organ player at the base of a sweeping staircase.

Why didn't Jerome want his ashes spread in a place like this?

Well, he was going to leave a bit of himself here whether he liked it or not.

She poured some of Jerome's ashes out in front of the locked entrance.

"What are you doing?" Janice shrieked.

"This is where Jerome and I had our first official date," Edie said. "He might have been more concerned with footballs and fiddles, but I'm going to leave some of him here whether he likes it or not."

She walked down the street a bit until she came to the Tennessee Theatre, but it wasn't open yet.

"Figures," she muttered as she poured a little more of Jerome around the ticket booth.

"Edie, please!"

"I don't want to be rude, but are we still going to get our scholarships since you're spreading ashes in other places?" Peyton asked.

Edie turned to her companions, feeling every one of her eighty-six years. "Who's going to tell? I'm not telling. Are you?"

She stared down each and every one of them until he or she gave a head shake to the negative.

"After we went to the old S&W on our date, we came here for a movie. It didn't look quite as nice back then. In fact, they'd pretty much given up live shows. I think we saw the first Sunday movie they ever played, some awful old thing with Errol Flynn. Oh, that movie was horrible, but the marriage that followed was incredible."

They all stood there for a few minutes longer. No one was willing to interrupt Edie's reverie. Janice reached into her pocketbook for a tissue and wiped a tear from her eye.

Then Edie snapped to. "I think we're going to do a hint of

tailgating, see if the Orange Blossom Special lives up to the hype. What do you think?"

***

A few minutes later, they'd managed to wedge the hearse into a spot at the Wesley Foundation parking lot. They didn't have any food, so the kids nestled in the back with the luggage while Janice and Edie sat in the camp chairs Edie had packed. An endless parade of people dressed in orange and white tromped up the hill.

Thinking of how Edie had fiercely spread Jerome's ashes at the old cafeteria and the theater, Janice knew there were some things she needed to say. Of course, knowing that she needed to say them and actually doing so were two different things. She'd have to swallow her pride, and she was pretty sure it was going to be bitter.

"Edie," Janice made herself say. "I'm sorry for the way I've treated you all of these years. I've come to see how much you loved Jerome."

Edie stared through her. Janice had hoped for a return apology, but she couldn't tell how the conversation was going to go. Well, in for a penny . . .

"I've been jealous of how you got to go off to college. That was wrong of me."

Edie swiped at her moist eyes. Janice didn't think she'd ever seen the woman cry before.

"Thank you. I'm sorry, too. I've been jealous of you, you know."

"How? Why?"

Edie choked on a sob. "Jerome and I always wanted kids."

Janice's breath caught in her throat. "You *wanted* to have children?"

Edie shot a glance at the two kids in the back of the hearse, each of her wrinkles etched with longing. "Very much. Never could make it happen like you and Harvey did."

"Why not?" Janice winced. She shouldn't have asked that question. She was stunned, and she felt an embarrassment of riches as she thought of her children and grandchildren, and even her great-grandchildren. Instead of being jealous of Edie, she should've been sharing her wealth.

Edie shook her head. "No one knows. I got to a point where it didn't bother me so much, but now that Jerome's gone, I'm just . . . alone."

Janice reached over and grabbed her sister-in-law's hand. "Oh, Edie. You're not alone. You have me and Harvey, and those knuckleheads taking a nap right over there in the back of our hearse."

Edie turned her gaze back to Janice, her eyes sparkling and warm. "I always wanted to be a mother like you. I often wished I had curves like yours, too."

"But I've been skipping desserts because I wanted to be thinner like you. I could've sworn you were trying to tempt me with how good your cakes and cookies always smelled."

"Really?"

"Really."

Jerome had been right. They could've been friends all of this time. Well, better late than never.

"Maybe . . . Maybe . . ." Janice struggled to get the words out through a constricted throat. "Maybe we should go to Hawaii like he said. I've always wanted to go, but I'd be afraid to fly alone."

Edie looked away. "I don't think it would be wise to make any long-term plans. Maybe you could take your daughter. Or one of the kids."

Janice's stomach flip-flopped. "Long-term plans? Are you sick?" Surely, she and Edie had not finally forged a tenuous truce only for Edie to be dying.

"No, but I don't want to stick around until I am, now, do I? I think I'll go inside and get a Coke. Want anything?"

Janice shook her head. She tried to puzzle through what Edie had just said. Was she saying what she thought she was saying? How did she know whether or not she was sticking around . . . unless . . .

No. She couldn't believe the strong, no-nonsense Edie would do something so stupid.

Then again, taking matters into her own hands sounded exactly like something Edie would do.

Not that Janice was going to let her.

"*M*an, this really is the ultimate tailgating machine!" Walter said from where he lay in the back of the hearse. He'd eaten the biggest breakfast the Cracker Barrel had, and he really wanted a nap.

"Walter, have you ever been to this stadium before? How are we going to do this?"

They lay on their sides looking at each other. Walter's gaze wanted to slide to Peyton's lips, but he made himself look her in the eye instead. "I don't know. I've been here before, and it's huge. I can't even describe it. You'll have to see it."

"We need to have a plan," she said. "Some kind of distraction."

"We could have Grandma and Aunt Edie get into an old lady catfight." Walter grinned at the thought of the two women swinging their purses at each other. Of course, if they hadn't come to blows yet on this trip, they probably weren't going to.

"Maybe we should do it for them."

What would it be like for him and Peyton to run across the field to the end zone? When he looked down, he was holding Peyton's hand. She had blushed a pretty pink.

He was thinking about kissing her. It wouldn't take much, since their faces were only inches apart. And no one would notice since they were in the shadowy interior of the hearse.

He took a deep breath and leaned toward Peyton. Just as his lips were about to touch hers, Aunt Edie grabbed his ankle and told him it was time to head over to the stadium.

In his shock, he let go of Peyton's hand, the spell of the moment broken.

And that was for the best, he told himself. The last thing he needed to do was get involved with a girl when he was headed off to college at the end of the school year. It didn't matter that she could kick his ass at soccer or that she had the prettiest freckles that spread like a constellation over her cheeks and nose.

Nope. It didn't matter at all.

***

Peyton couldn't catch her breath. She'd come within inches of her very first kiss. She'd been so nervous about lying in the back of the hearse, but Walter was there, so she wanted to be, too. And it hadn't been that bad! She had to admit that hearses didn't frighten her anymore, especially not if she was with him.

As for her almost-kiss? She couldn't decide if she was mad at Miss Edie or grateful.

"You kids are in for a treat," the offending party said as she led them up the hill and away from the Wesley Foundation.

"Why's that?" asked Peyton.

"This stadium holds over a hundred thousand people."

"What the—?" asked Peyton.

"Why in the blue blazes did Jerome want us to do this?" added Janice, huffing as she struggled to climb the hill. "I feel packed in like a sardine in this crowd. What are we supposed to do if there's some kind of terrorist attack like back in 2001?

There's no way they can effectively move all of these people out of here quickly."

"Hush, you," Miss Edie said, but her voice was softer than it had been. "Look! The band's about to round the corner down there by the new library. Let's hurry!"

Miss Edie moved deceptively fast for a lady of her age, but at least they were going downhill at this point. They stopped in front of a huge building that had to be the library and watched as the biggest marching band Peyton had ever seen rounded the corner while playing "Rocky Top."

Once the band passed, Peyton and her companions followed the swell of the crowd down one hill and up another. She kinda loved it here. She wanted to be a part of this excitement. Maybe she really did want to go to college.

They brandished their tickets and shuffled into the stadium like sheep, wandering the outer edges of the building until they found the correct portal. Peyton stepped out into the sun and gasped at the sheer enormity of the place. Over a hundred thousand people, Miss Edie had said.

"That's like all the people in Ellery times twenty," Peyton murmured.

"Told you you'd have to see it," Walter said with a grin. He looked so handsome that Peyton felt a twinge of remorse that she hadn't gotten that kiss after all. It would've made a great story for her children one day.

"I'm gonna feel weird sitting in the Vanderbilt section," she said.

"Well, those are the tickets we have," Miss Edie said primly. "So, that is where we will sit."

They slowly and carefully picked their way to their seats. Mr. Little had somehow managed to get them front-row seats.

"Would you look at that," Walter said.

"What?" Peyton asked.

"See that usher? He's standing right in front of a set of steps that will take you all the way down to the field. These are some lucky seats, considering what we're here to do."

Peyton surveyed the situation. They sat low in a wedge of the stadium reserved for fans of the visiting team, with the Vanderbilt band too close for her liking, but she couldn't imagine being any closer to the field. Luck? She was beginning to wonder if there was such a thing as luck.

The Tennessee band sat on the same side of the stadium but in the opposite corner. They played loudly, their brash trumpets bouncing off the empty seats. The Vanderbilt band played their fight song at the same time, and cacophony reigned for a few minutes.

Her first live football game, a chance to go to college, and she'd almost gotten her first kiss.

Thank you, Mr. Jerome.

*I*t was chillier than Edie would've liked, and she noticed Janice had folded up on herself, her now-bare legs no doubt susceptible to the cold. She called Walter over and whispered, "Could you be a dear and see if you could buy a blanket and a sweatshirt for your grandmother? Maybe buy some extras for all of us?"

Walter's eyes almost popped out of their sockets as she handed him a wad of twenties. He didn't know how expensive things were in the stadium. He also didn't know this was her last hurrah—she'd decided that when Janice asked her to go to Hawaii. Maybe she should speak with Ben about divvying up her estate among the three of them when she was gone, maybe make the ridiculous request that Peyton go to Hawaii with Janice or some such. Making crazy behests had worked for Jerome, after all.

By the time Walter returned with a sweatshirt, four blankets, four Cokes, and a cup of chili and chips called a Petro, the section around them had filled in. Someone of the Vandy fans grumbled to have so much orange in their midst. Edie bit her tongue.

"What's this?" Janice asked.

"I sent Walter to get you a sweatshirt and a blanket for your naked legs," Edie said.

Janice made a face from her seat on the other side of the kids, but then she said, "Thank you."

"Peyton, would you please pass me a Coke?" Edie asked.

The girl dutifully passed the beverage down, but someone was tapping on Edie's shoulder. "Are those kids named Walter and Peyton?"

"Yes."

"Like the Chicago running back?"

Edie stared at him blankly. "Who?"

"Aw, man, why didn't I think of that before?" Walter asked with a grin. "Hey, Peyton. We're 'Sweetness.'"

"What are you talking about?"

Walter rolled his eyes and launched into a discussion about some Chicago Bears running back and of his yards received, his consecutive games played, and his being chosen man of the year. Edie looked up to the man who'd tapped her on the shoulder. "Now look what you've done."

"I thought it was pretty cool." He shrugged and extended his hand. "Name's Danny."

"Nice to meet you, Danny. I'm Edie."

Despite such a pleasant beginning, what came next stressed them all out. Tennessee took the lead in the first, but Vandy answered in the second. It was a messy game with five turnovers. Even worse, with six minutes to go in the fourth, it looked as though Tennessee was going to blow it once again, since they'd just kicked off to Vandy.

"Not again," Walter moaned, his voice hoarse from yelling.

Janice motioned for him to switch seats with her then leaned over to Edie. "We've got to do something. The game is almost over."

"'We'?"

"Of course, 'we'! Jerome wouldn't have had it any other way."

Edie knew. She'd been clutching the ibuprofen bottle full of his ashes since halftime. "I don't know what to do," she said. "How do I get past that usher?"

"You should send the kids."

Edie thought about it. They were young and fast, but they also didn't need a criminal record so early in their lives. "No. I don't want them to get into trouble. I'll go. What does it matter if I go to jail?"

"What does it matter?!" Janice shrieked.

Danny leaned forward. "Why are you talking about going to jail?"

Edie took a deep breath and gave him the short version of the story: Her husband was dead and wanted his ashes scattered in one of Tennessee's end zones. Their new friend Danny was so engrossed in what she was saying that he even forgot to cheer for Vandy once or twice.

"Maybe me and the boys can help," Danny said.

About that time Tennessee intercepted the ball and ran it almost all the way back. The crowd roared, but it was a nervous energy. Vandy still had two minutes to answer.

Danny turned to his compatriots and whispered something, and the game of telephone continued down the row and then to the one above it.

"What did you tell them?" Edie asked.

"I told them that one of y'all was going to do something as a distraction and that we were all to stand up and point."

"But I don't know what the distraction will be!" Edie yelled. She looked over her shoulder nervously. Thankfully, the usher guarding the steps to the field hadn't been able to hear her over the noise made when they announced that Tennessee's touchdown would stand.

Danny shrugged. "Ask the kids."

As overtime started, Edie, Janice, Walter, and Peyton formed their own huddle.

"I'm going to need a distraction," Edie said as the Vandy fans went wild about something that was happening on the field.

"I'm going with you," Janice said.

"Fine. *We* are going to need a distraction."

"Peyton and I should do this, Aunt Edie," Walter said.

"No, dear. You two do *not* need to go to jail."

He hesitated. "What do you want us to do?"

"Think of something, and think of it quickly," Edie said. She looked up to see that Vandy was only eleven yards away from winning the game. But then . . .

Interception! Tennessee had the ball back.

The stadium exploded, Vandy players started to leave while Tennessee players rushed the field, but the officials called them all back to their places as the last play was under review. The entire stadium held its breath because Tennessee had been robbed many times at the end of a game recently, their fortunes rising and falling like a ridiculous roller coaster.

Edie clutched the ibuprofen bottle in her hand. She needed a Tennessee win, something to get the whole crowd going. *Come on, Jerome, can you talk to God about this one? If God's not available, what about your precious general?*

The usher was watching the screen to see what the outcome would be, and Edie edged to the opening that led out to the field. Janice followed.

The official up on the big screen announced that the ruling on the field would stand and threw up two arms. The stadium exploded with cheers, and even the usher pumped his fist. Edie started sneaking down the stairs with Janice hot on her heels, looking anything but incognito in the new orange sweatshirt with her suit and heels.

"Hey, what do you—?"

But then the section behind her howled and whistled. The

usher looked back at them, and Edie ran as fast as her legs could carry her, practically dragging Janice through a sea of football players. In the corner of her eye, she could see policemen running toward her, and her fingers fumbled with the top to the ibuprofen bottle.

It came open, the lid flying away from her, and she moved to dump the ashes in the same instant a policeman grabbed her arm. The ashes flew in a graceful arc, some landing on jubilant Volunteers and others landing on Jerome's beloved checker-board end zone.

Then her arm was being drawn behind her back, and she was being told that she had the right to remain silent. "Officer, is this really necessary?"

"Sir, we are just two crazy old ladies," Janice was saying. "We'll come along peacefully."

He looked at the two women dubiously but nodded his head that they should follow. Edie looked for Walter and Peyton in the crowd, finally spotting where they waved wildly. She grabbed Janice's hand and threw it up as if they were champions, and everyone in that section of the stadium cheered.

When she lowered their arms, she continued to clasp Janice's hand. Whatever the Knoxville PD had in store for them, she and Janice would face it together, and she had to appreciate a friend who was willing to do that for her.

A few minutes earlier

"*H*ey, what do you—?"

Peyton had to do something. She stood up on the metal bench, grabbed Walter's cheeks, and kissed him, pressing her lips to his, hard, because she didn't know what else to do. The Vanderbilt fans around them went wild. She opened one eye long enough to see that the usher had been distracted by them just long enough to let Miss Edie and Miss Janice get past him. She backed away from Walter and looked up just as Miss Edie made it to the end zone, Miss Janice huffing behind her.

As the cops closed in on them, the entire section, Vandy and Tennessee fans alike, jumped up and down and cheered for the older ladies. When they saw Edie's hand wave and a hint of gray dust, then they really went wild. Peyton jumped down from the metal bench and hugged Walter. Then, when Miss Edie held up Miss Janice's hand as if they were the tag team champions of the world, they all went nuts again.

"Guess we're going to have to call Mr. Little and figure out how to bail them out, huh?" she said, turning to face Walter. He stared at her so intensely, she wondered if he had ever looked away.

"Why did you do that?" he asked.

What could she tell him? That she couldn't think of anything more distracting than him? That she had a major crush on him? That—

"When we were back in the hearse, I thought you might kiss me. And then I realized I wanted you to kiss me, so it was the most distracting thing I could think of to do."

"Really."

Was he mad?

"So, you don't make a habit of kissing boys at football games?"

She looked down at her orange Chucks. "Actually, that was the very first time."

He lifted her chin. "Well, that explains your lack of technique, then."

Jerk.

Embarrassed, she smacked his shoulder and moved away. He grabbed for her, but then he let his hands drop, fisted at his sides.

"I'm sorry that didn't come out the way I meant for it to." He drew in a ragged breath. "You took me by surprise."

She turned to look at him, glad he'd reached for her but also glad he'd thought better of it. "What *did* you mean, then?"

"I meant that I don't think that should count as a first kiss, you know, since it was really meant to be more of a distraction." He took a step closer, pausing to see whether she would move away. She didn't, just as she hadn't gone easy on him when they'd played soccer the day before yesterday, a day that felt like a lifetime ago.

"Then, why don't you show me what a first kiss should look like?"

As the Tennessee band played a subdued "Tennessee Waltz," Walter leaned in and did just that.

"*D*on't you two look stylish in your matching ankle bracelets?"

Edie looked up to see Walter coming through the back door. She stopped arguing with Janice about how she shouldn't wear pumps to Hawaii and went to embrace him. "Have you grown taller?"

"A little," he said with a shy smile.

"All packed for UT training camp?"

"Yes, ma'am," he said, his smile widening to a grin. "Gonna try to have a better season than last year."

"I'm more worried about your academics," Janice said as she moved in for a hug of her own.

"I still can't believe they put you on house arrest," Walter said.

"And I had never been in trouble with the law a day in my life," moaned Janice for the thousandth time. "Just my luck we'd get a hanging judge."

"Oh, come off it. The ankle bracelets come off tomorrow. Better than jail time."

"It *should* have been probation," Janice muttered.

The door opened behind Walter, and Peyton came in. "How's the packing going?"

"I don't know," Edie asked, eyebrow arched. "How's the ACT studying going?"

"I made a twenty-nine on my last math practice test," she said shyly.

"That's great!"

"Walter helped, too," she said.

Edie looked at the two wistfully.

"I was wondering if you wanted me to drive you to the airport day after tomorrow," Walter asked.

"That would be rather thoughtful of you," Janice said.

"Can I come, too?" Peyton asked.

"Sure," said Edie, pulling the girl in for a side hug. "That reminds me. I picked up a little math practice book for you at the library. Let me get it."

She stepped into the darkened dining room and turned to see the light from the kitchen seeping around the swinging door. Janice laughed at something, and Peyton shrieked with laughter in response. When she pushed back through the doorway, her heart closed up a little because Walter was leading Peyton through the steps of a waltz in the kitchen, humming as he did.

"Where'd you learn to do that?" Janice asked.

"Mom made me do that crazy cotillion thing, remember?"

The two made another tiny twirl, and Peyton looked up at Walter with so much love that Edie's eyes glazed over with tears.

"Excuse me," she said, racing back to the bathroom. She took her bottle of pills, that magic combination she'd researched with the help of that Compassion and Choices organization. She'd held on to them over the past few months, not quite as ready to leave because Janice kept coming up with things for them to do.

Like this Hawaii trip.

Surely Janice hadn't figured out her plan. Surely her former nemesis hadn't been keeping her busy on purpose.

Someone lightly tapped on the door.

"You okay, Edie?"

Yes, Edie decided, Janice had figured her out. The woman had always been smarter than Edie had given her credit for being. She thought of how Jerome had wanted his ashes spread in all those places that didn't really have anything to do with her. Well, she was entitled to a few memories of her own, too. Before she could change her mind, Edie poured the pills into the toilet and flushed it. She made a show of running water to wash her hands, then she used her most tart tone of voice to say, "I was trying out your way of dilly-dallying in the restroom," as she opened the door.

"The kids are sorry if they upset you," Janice said.

"They didn't upset me. They reminded me of Jerome," Edie said wistfully. She told the kids that when she went back to the kitchen, then she served up pineapple cake and coffee for everyone. This time Janice had a slice, and it did Edie's heart good to watch her friend's eyes close in delight as she allowed herself one of life's little treats.

"Hey, Miss Edie?"

"Yes, Peyton, dear?"

"Could we take you to the airport in the hearse? You know, for old times' sake?"

Edie started to say no, but she looked around the room at people who kept showing up when they didn't have to. She heard herself say, "I wouldn't have it any other way."

Did you enjoy *Orange Blossom Special*? Please feel free to leave an honest review at any retailer or on Goodreads. That's a great way to earn a star for your celestial crown.

NOW TREAT YOURSELF TO THE
FIRST CHAPTER OF BLESS HER
HEART...

Chapter 1

*T*here were only three words in the English language
that I hated with all of my being: *bless, your,* and *heart*
—specifically in that order. One look through the glass door
that led to Love Ministries, and I knew those words were
winging my way. Miss Georgette wrestled with the door,
pushing when she ought to pull. She came to the little brick
building twice every week, but she still had trouble with that
door. Today, the older lady wore a knit pantsuit with a cat
appliqué on the front. Siamese cat earrings dangled from her
ears.

"Why, Posey. Are you *still* working as a receptionist?"

"Yes, ma'am." Just as I had for the past five years.

"Well."

Don't say it. Don't say it. Don't say it.

"Bless your heart."

My entire body relaxed. I'd braced myself for her words as
one would brace for bullets when standing in front of a firing
squad. She'd said them. It was done.

"You know, I still say you would've made a right fine elementary teacher. I was so disappointed when you didn't take a job after you graduated."

"I am sorry about that," I said. Mainly sorry for myself, but sorry nonetheless.

She continued speaking as if she hadn't heard me. "You were one of my absolute best students when I taught elementary education at the college. I still have some of the games and projects that you made."

Miss Georgette reminded me of this every time she came through the doors. While flattered that she still had some of my school projects, I wished she wouldn't remind me that my life hadn't exactly gone as planned. At thirty-two years old, I was supposed to be almost ten years into a teaching career with at least two children. I had d) none of the above.

"I heard from Lisa who heard from Jackie that Heather Mickens has been put on bed rest so they have a supply position open in first grade. You should apply and see how you like it."

Here was a first: Miss Georgette actually pushing me in the direction of a teaching job instead of bemoaning the fact I didn't have one. "Oh, I don't know. I bet I've forgotten everything I once knew. The standards have probably changed, and—"

"Pish-posh. First graders are the same as they ever were." Miss Georgette waved away my concerns, and the siamese cats hanging from her ear dangled in time to the motion. "You should apply for the job and at least see what happens. Ellery Elementary won't find a more upstanding lady than you."

I looked down at my floral dress with the lace collar. I spent a lot of time cultivating my image as "upstanding" because everyone knew my mother had a bit of a past. Sure, I might dress like an extra on *The Golden Girls* now, but I was the daughter of the legendary hippie girl who ran away from home and came back pregnant. I was the baby she bore, a girl who'd never known a father. Never mind the fact I had nothing to do with my mother's actions. They, of course, were all reasons to bless my heart.

I could still hear the voices, the whispered snatches of conversation from the teachers and professors as I made my way through Ellery Elementary then through the local college and beyond, always doing my best to be invisible.

Her mama makes her clothes out of hemp instead of getting them at the store.

Well, bless her heart.

No clue who her father is. Vonda over at the Health Department saw the birth certificate and said no father was listed.

That's awful. Bless her heart.

Did you hear her mama's got pregnant again? Still not married.

Mmm-hmm. Bless her heart.

Now she's married that Chad Love. He has to be at least ten years older than she is.

Oh, Bless her heart.

They've been married forever now and still no kids. Think something's wrong with one of them?

Probably her. Poor thing, bless her heart.

Miss Georgette waved a beefy hand in front of my face. "Did you hear me, Posey?"

"No, ma'am. I'm sorry. I remembered some things I had to do." I made a show of making notes on my planner then looked up. "What were you saying?"

"I was saying you should apply for the supply position, and that I would be happy to put in a good word for you if you did."

"That's really kind of you, Miss Georgette."

The tips of her ears and the tops of her cheeks turned pink. "It would be nothing. My pleasure, really."

"Well, I appreciate it." Surprisingly, I did. Aside from the constant heart-blessing, Miss Georgette had always been very good to me.

"Don't you forget to turn in that application," she admonished as she started down the hall toward her weekly Bible study.

Unlikely that I would forget. Even more unlikely that I would turn in the application. Chad didn't want me to work outside the home. When we first married, the plan was for me to stay home and be mother to our children. He promised me at least two even though I wanted four. God, however, had other plans. After ten years of trying to get pregnant, I hadn't once had a positive pregnancy test. We'd been to a few doctors even though Chad wanted to leave everything to God's will. The last doctor told me I would never conceive. I tried to mean it when I prayed "thy will be done," but I couldn't help but add a plea for motherhood. God did change his mind once or twice, right?

After the doctor's pronouncement, I asked Chad about adoption. He said he didn't feel comfortable having some stranger's baby in his house. That hurt my heart. Then I asked about teaching again, but he always found a way to talk me out of it. Funny that I, the daughter of Ellery's most notorious single mom, would allow a man to talk me out of anything, but we'd left the Baptist Church about two years into our marriage to form a ministry that relied on the principle of men being the head of their respective households. Wives, of course, were to be cherished in addition to being submissive. I had to admit it was quite freeing not to have to make any decisions.

Even so, I chafed at having to wait for his blessing—or God's —to do what I wanted to do.

It can't hurt to look for an application.

I booted up my computer and searched for the Yessum County School System, the online application taunting me. Since I obviously wouldn't be having babies any time soon, at least I could teach them. This receptionist job was supposed to have been temporary. Not enough people came through the door to merit my existence anyway. Sometimes I wondered how Chad kept the doors open, but, as head of the household, he handled all of the finances so I took it on faith that he had everything under control. Submission and obedience, as he was fond of reminding me, were more difficult than his position of authority and responsibility.

Down the hall behind me Chad whistled as he approached. I quickly switched tabs to a document before he could see the application. He didn't like for me to be on the Internet. He said he was afraid I'd stumble upon something impure. Well, it *was* the Internet.

"Posey, are all of my Bible study members here?" he asked, leaning over my desk with a smile that didn't quite reach his eyes.

"They're all here," I said.

Still he leaned, studying me so I took a moment to study him. My husband looked more handsome now than he had before: dark hair and brown eyes with crinkles at the edges. Sometimes I wondered how he had ended up with a plain girl like me, but he could talk almost anyone into anything, and I was no exception. He'd sold me on the American dream: nice house and two and a half kids, even joking that he didn't know how we'd make that half. I suggested a dog instead, but he reminded me he was allergic.

Then he'd sold me on submission, pointing out that, without a father, my home life had been less than ideal. He was right about that. Granny and Mom had argued. Often they had no extra money to go around. Thanks to Mom's less than disciplined behavior, I'd had my heart blessed more times than I could count. I couldn't argue with him that she would've benefited from the discipline that seemingly eluded her until she'd had her third child.

Chad was all about discipline. If I spent too much on groceries, then he took away some of my pin money to remind me to be more frugal. If I overindulged and my pants got too tight, he hid the cookies. If I got behind with clerical tasks or domestic chores, then he had me stay late an hour at work or had me get up an hour earlier on Saturday to make up for lost time. Sometimes I muttered under my breath at his "suggestions," but I did have to admit that we stayed on budget, I stayed in my pants, and everything ran smoothly at home and at work. In that way, he'd given me the stability I'd always craved.

At least he'd never actually raised his hand to me even though some of the ministers he communicated with did take the ideas of submissive wives and discipline quite literally.

Well, there was that one time, but I'd mad him understand there were two things I wouldn't tolerate: being hit and infidelity. I'd given him one more chance on the first, but there were no extra chances on the second.

"Posey, dear?"

"Yes?"

"You were daydreaming again," he said as he chucked my chin. "Would you be a dear and go to the Calais Cafe to get us lunch today?" He slid his glasses back up his nose.

"Of course," I said, "Do we have enough money in the checking account, though."

"Always thinking, you," he said as he reached for his wallet and took out a couple of twenties. "You know what I like. Be sure to bring back the change, though."

"I'll have it by noon."

He kissed my cheek then headed down the hall still whistling. How was it possible that he didn't seem to age at all, but I couldn't keep the ravages of time at bay? Today would be another day to skip dessert or anything fatty because my shapewear was cutting into me again. He had that dignified sprinkle of gray at his temple, but my dark brown hair threatened to go salt and pepper any day now. He still wore the same pant size as when we got married, but my hips kept spreading.

They looked like child-bearing hips. Oh, the irony.

While Chad talked to the old ladies down the hall about

Revelation for the umpteenth dozen time, I created a new email address and then filled out the application to be a supply teacher. It felt sneaky to do so, but Chad insisted that we share email addresses, and I wasn't ready to tell him yet. It was worth whatever lecture he might give me to be able to surprise him with something I'd done for the good of our family.

As penance, I determined I would get him dessert even though I wouldn't be having any. Once at the Calais Cafe, I knew he wanted the chicken pot pie and a slice of pecan pie. Finding something healthy for myself would be more difficult. After looking over the menu, I settled on a chicken caesar salad with light Italian dressing on the side. They had a pristine chocolate pie in the safe, uncut with mile-high meringue that had browned just so. My mouth watered, but I passed.

Once I returned I thought we might lunch together, but Chad told me he needed to take a working lunch. "Oh, you got me pie, too! How thoughtful of you."

This earned me a kiss on the lips and a covert pinch on the butt once he was sure no one was looking. Then he took his lunch to the back, and I sat down at my lonely reception desk to convince myself that I did, indeed, like chicken caesar salad.

My self wasn't having it that day.

When Amanda Kildare appeared on the other side of the door, teary eyed and looking both ways, I wasn't sad about pushing the salad to the side. Amanda and I had gone to school together, but we hadn't moved in the same circles. She had been popular. Me? Not so much. Even so, she'd started coming to me for advice when she and her husband jumped ship from First Baptist to attend Love Ministries. I didn't like giving advice, but Chad had told me to say a quick prayer and offer up what words I could because he wasn't an expert on those things women discussed.

I suppose my staid *Golden Girls* aesthetic inspired confidence.

Next time I knew, she stood over my desk wringing her hands. "Everything okay, Amanda?"

"No. Not really. I see you're eating lunch, but could I talk to you for a few minutes? I need some advice."

"Sure, but Chad's just down the hall."

She hesitated and looked toward his office as though afraid he would appear. "Really, this is something that needs to be discussed woman-to-woman."

"It's not gossip, right?" I was so not in the mood to hear the gossip passage from Romans later.

"No, no. This is about me."

"Well, I'll help you if I can," I said.

If I'd been hoping for something quickly discussed over the reception desk, I was destined for disappointment. Amanda went across the little lobby to drag an overstuffed chair behind the desk. It got hung between the desk and the wall, so she stepped over and sat down, leaning over her knees. She smelled of Chanel Number Five, with every golden hair in place and her sweater set just so. Her tiny little boots tapped on the floor, the perfect shade of brown and the perfect style for her designer jeans. No matter how many times she came through the door, I couldn't help but marvel at what brought the former Homecoming Queen to me.

Finally, she whispered, "You know *that* book?"

Heavens. That again? I had a pretty good idea where this was going, but I cautiously asked, "Which book?"

Amanda reached behind her for what had to be a designer hand bag and opened it enough for me to see. Sure enough, it was, indeed, *that* book, the gray one with the tie on the cover.

"I know of the book."

He eyes gleamed with hope. "Have you read it?"

"No, should I?"

Her shoulders slumped. "You're going to judge me, too."

"Amanda, you know I wouldn't do that. Judge not lest ye be judged."

She took a deep breath and launched into her story, a variation of which I'd been hearing for months. She'd been curious, wanting to see what all of the fuss was about. She'd asked her husband to try some new things in the bedroom. I mentally placed my bets for who'd upset her: Husband? Friend? Aunt? Sister?

"And then he told his mother!"

I did not see that one coming.

"As if I weren't already embarrassed enough that he was telling his mother about our sex life, she told me I was going to hell for reading such filth. Do you think I'm going to hell, Posey?"

Ah, the million dollar question. At least ten different women had been in my office over the past few months, all wanting to know if I thought they were going to hell for reading a book. "Tell me, Amanda, have you killed anyone recently?"

"No," she said with a sniff.

"Stolen from anyone? Maybe disrespected your parents or coveted your neighbor's husband?"

"No! Ew."

"Did this book make you commit adultery?"

"You know it didn't."

"Maybe you made a graven image or took up satanism?"

She gasped, "What has gotten into you?"

Even as she said it, all of my examples dawned on her. "Oh. I get it. You're saying that I haven't caused anyone harm so it's okay."

I shrugged. "There's a difference between 'okay' and 'good.' There's that whole passage about thinking on what's pure and lovely and admirable, but I don't think reading a book is going to send you to hell. Unless it has to do with devil worship."

She graced me with the homecoming smile that had

launched a thousand votes. "Thank you, Posey. You know, I would feel better, though, if you would read the book and then tell me it's okay."

"No, thank you. I don't really have much time for reading." *At least not for things that I don't want to read.*

"Well, I'm done with this book, so I'll leave it here with you." She took the book in question and put it in my bottom drawer.

"Amanda—"

"No, I trust you to get rid of it," she said with that beaming smile. "Thank you so much for making me feel better."

"I didn't really do that much," I said. "I still think you should've spoken with Chad. He's the preacher."

She dragged the chair back to where it belonged and turned to look at me with her expression all scrunched up. "No. He would've given me the lecture about asking my husband permission for what I read or something like that. You give better advice because you help people figure things out for themselves rather than just telling them what to do."

I didn't have an answer for that, but I wished I had someone who'd help me figure things out without telling me what to do. I opened my mouth to say "You're welcome," but Amanda was already gone.

I could still see her book from where she didn't close the drawer all the way, so I slammed it shut.

Wanna keep reading? You can buy *Bless Her Heart* here.

ABOUT THE AUTHOR

Born and raised in a small town in West Tennessee, Sally Kilpatrick writes to go home. She lives with her husband, a Georgia boy, and her two kids in Marietta, Georgia, but her heart has never left Tennessee, and her books reflect the small-town shenanigans and memorable characters she grew up around. Her latest novel, Oh My Stars, was described by RT Book Reviews as written in a way that "makes readers feel as if they are hanging out with their best friend." With five novels under her belt, Sally has won multiple awards, including the 2018 and 2019 Georgia Author of the Year, the Maggie Award of Excellence, the Booksellers' Best, and the 2016 Nancy Knight Award for Mentorship. Visit her author website at sallykilpatrick.com or follow her on Twitter as @SuperWriterMom.

Connect with Sally online:
Goodreads: https://www.goodreads.com/author/show/6906076.Sally_Kilpatrick

Fiction From the Heart: https://www.facebook.com/groups/FictionFromTheHeart/

facebook.com/SuperWriterMom
twitter.com/SuperWriterMom
bookbub.com/authors/sally-kilpatrick

CPSIA information can be obtained
at www.ICGtesting.com
Printed in the USA
FSHW010953020221
78258FS